RALPH COMPTON: THE AMARILLO TRAIL

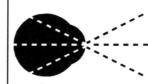

This Large Print Book carries the
Seal of Approval of N.A.V.H.

RALPH COMPTON: THE AMARILLO TRAIL

JORY SHERMAN

THORNDIKE PRESS

A part of Gale, Cengage Learning

GALE
CENGAGE Learning·

Detroit • New York • San Francisco • New Haven, Conn • Waterville, Maine • London

GALE
CENGAGE Learning·

LIBRARY OF CONGRESS CATALOGING-IN-PUBLICATION DATA

Sherman, Jory.
  The Amarillo trail / by Jory Sherman. — Large print ed.
    p. cm. — (Thorndike Press large print western)
  At head of title: Ralph Compton
  "A Ralph Compton Novel."
  ISBN-13: 978-1-4104-4301-4(hardcover)
  ISBN-10: 1-4104-4301-9(hardcover)
  1. Cattle drives—Fiction. 2. Brothers—Fiction. 3. Large type books.
  I. Title. II. Title: Ralph Compton.
  PS3569.H43A83 2011
  813'.54—dc23   2011034124

Published in 2011 by arrangement with NAL Signet, a member of Penguin Group (USA) Inc.

Printed in the United States of America
1 2 3 4 5 6 7 15 14 13 12 11

THE IMMORTAL COWBOY

This is respectfully dedicated to the "American Cowboy." His was the saga sparked by the turmoil that followed the Civil War, and the passing of more than a century has by no means diminished the flame.

True, the old days and the old ways are but treasured memories, and the old trails have grown dim with the ravages of time, but the spirit of the cowboy lives on.

In my travels — to Texas, Oklahoma, Kansas, Nebraska, Colorado, Wyoming, New Mexico, and Arizona — I always find something that reminds me of the Old West. While I am walking these plains and mountains for the first time, there is this feeling that a part of me is eternal, that I have known these old trails before. I believe it is the undying spirit of the frontier calling me, through the mind's eye, to step back into time. What is the appeal of the Old West of the American frontier?

It has been epitomized by some as the dark and bloody period in American history. Its heroes — Crockett, Bowie, Hickok, Earp — have been reviled and criticized. Yet the Old West lives on, larger than life.

It has become a symbol of freedom, when there was always another mountain to climb and another river to cross; when a dispute between two men was settled not with expensive lawyers, but with fists, knives, or guns. Barbaric? Maybe. But some things never change. When the cowboy rode into the pages of American history, he left behind a legacy that lives within the hearts of us all.

— Ralph Compton

CHAPTER 1

Delmer Jasper Blaine bent over the pommel of his saddle, bracing himself against the brunt of the fierce Amarillo wind. Riding alongside him, a red bandanna pasted against his face from nose to neck, was the agent from Salina, Kansas, Alvin Mortenson, his hat brim pulled down over his slitted eyes so that he resembled a highwayman or a bank robber.

"Is it always this windy, Mr. Blaine?" Mortenson yelled into the teeth of the wind.

"Call me Doc. Nope, some days it blows real hard here."

Mortenson snorted as he looked at the rippling grass, the white-faced cattle grazing, their rumps to the wind. He was a lean, wiry man in his forties, with a bristly mustache, close-set hazel eyes, and a chiseled face with high, sharp cheekbones and a thin, elongated nose that came to a point just above his upper lip. He wore a pale yellow chambray shirt and light corduroy trousers tucked into a pair of worn cowhand boots. A knotted bandanna ringed his throat and his small Stetson crowned a slightly balding pate.

"If I'da knowed it would blow like this, I'd've carried a couple of bricks in my pockets."

"Last feller what done that wound up being stoned to death when the bricks were plucked from his pockets and follered him clear to Palo Duro Canyon at better'n a hundred miles an hour."

"All your cattle that fat, Doc?"

"These are the lean ones," Blaine said.

"I don't see three thousand head," Mortenson said.

"I got three ranches. My two sons run the other two. You got a month to spare, I'll show you ever' head."

"I got a long ride, Doc. First to Wichita to report to Mr. Fenster, then back to Dallas, where I live."

"So you'll take my word on this deal?"

"I'm leanin' that way. I see cattle in the distance and you say you've got better'n three thousand acres here. The other ranges are bigger'n this one, I take it."

"Yep, my son Jared runs a spread up to Perryton, and runs better'n two thousand head. Miles, my other son, is down to Dumas with more'n five thousand acres and he'll run in another fifteen hundred head for this drive."

"So your whole family is in this," Mortenson said.

"My sons will make the drive with their hands. I got a sick sister to tend to. They're good hands themselves and growed up with Herefords."

"Quite a family, Doc. Okay, let's go back to your house and I'll draw up the papers. Can you guarantee delivery by the first of June?"

"Sure can. It ain't but a hop, skip, and a jump to Salina. Plenty of water along the way."

"You'll be the first from this part of the country. Most of the cattle drives have been over the Goodnight-Loving Trail from deep down in Texas."

"Then we'll call ours the Amarillo Trail, Mortenson."

Mortenson laughed. "Good name for it," he said.

The two men rode back to Blaine's house, their backs peppered with grit from the strong western Texas wind. Doc was a square-shouldered man with a broad-beamed chest and powerful arms. He wasn't

9

a tall man, but was all muscle, with fierce blue eyes, shoulder-length hair, a prominent nose the size of a hammerhead, and a dripping blond mustache that matched his curly hair. He rode a steeldust gray horse named Sandy. Mortenson rode his own horse.

Blaine turned his horse off the path they had taken to view the cattle.

"Where we goin'?" Mortenson asked.

"Somethin' I got to see," Blaine said. "Promised the boys I'd stop by."

He headed Sandy toward a grove of oak and hickory trees standing just beyond a shallow arroyo. Voices drifted toward them on the wind, and as they drew closer, Mortensen saw some men on horseback, two standing on the ground, looking their way.

Blaine rode up, nodded to the men who raised their hands in greeting.

One man was seated on a bareback horse, his hands tied behind his back. There was a noose around his neck, the knot nestled against his neck. He looked Hispanic and scared.

"We're ready, boss," one man said to Blaine.

"What is this?" Mortenson asked.

"Horse thief," Blaine said. "We caught him late last night. He stole three horses from me."

"You goin' to hang him?" Mortenson said.

"That's the law," Blaine said. "We caught him red-handed."

"But shouldn't you take him to Amarillo, let him stand trial, speak his piece before a judge?"

"No need," Blaine said. "We caught him red-handed. Stealin' horses is a hangin' offense."

"I know, but —"

"No buts about it, Mortenson." Blaine looked at a man standing behind the saddleless horse.

"Okay, Freddie," he said.

Freddie, who was holding a quirt, lifted it high above his head and came down with it, hard. The three strands of leather smacked the horse's rump and it jumped, then bolted out from under the Mexican horse thief. Another hand caught the horse by its bridle and brought it to a halt.

There was a crack as the hangman's knot broke the man's neck. He was dead within seconds, his body swinging back and forth, twirling slowly beneath the live oak that had served as the hanging tree.

"My God. May God save his soul," Mortenson said, bowing his head.

Blaine lifted his head.

"Cut him down after a minute or two, Freddie," he said. "Cut him down and bury him."

"Yes, sir," Freddie said, and joined the other men in conversation. Blaine turned his horse.

"Now we can go to the house and look over those agreements, Mortenson."

"I could use a drink."

"Well, it's never too early for liquor when there's business to be done."

"No, I reckon not," Mortenson said.

He looked back over his shoulder. Two men on horseback were cutting the rope while two others stood waiting for the body to fall. Another pair of men stood by, leaning on shovels.

Mortenson shuddered.

He knew it was the law, unwritten probably, all over the West. But he had never seen justice meted out in that fashion. It was all so impersonal, so final.

And he couldn't get the image of that Mexican suddenly jerked off the horse and dangling there, his legs kicking with futility as his neck snapped.

He shuddered and looked at Blaine.

There was no change in the man, no visible sign that he was disturbed by the hanging of a living man. In fact, Doc Blaine was smiling and waving to his wife, Ethyl, who stood on the porch waiting for them. She was smiling too, and Mortenson wondered if she knew about the hanging.

"Did you send the horse thief on his way, Delmer?" she said as they rode up to the hitch rail.

"Done and done," Blaine said.

"I made a pot of coffee for you boys," she said. "And the liquor cabinet's open."

She went into the house as the two men dismounted. Sandy snorted and stood hip-shot. The horse switched his tail, swiping at small squadrons of blowflies.

It was not yet noon and the sun beat down as the wind gusted and ebbed like some invisible spirit, whipping up whirligigs of dust and whining in the eaves of the house like some lost Mexican soul.

CHAPTER 2

Mortenson sat at the kitchen table with Doc Blaine, legal papers spread out between them. Ethyl hovered over them like a cowbird in a herd of cattle, hopping between them with offers of more coffee or more fresh-baked cookies. The two men took what she offered, but kept their whiskey glasses filled as if to ward her off the small domain they had staked out for themselves.

"Lordy, Mr. Mortenson, I never heard such a ruckus as what we had last night," Ethyl gabbled as Mortenson pointed out clauses in the contract and places where Doc should sign. "I rousted Doc out of bed and told him something or somebody was gettin' at the horses."

"That when the horse thief was here, Mrs. Blaine?"

"Yes, sir, but it was Dusty's barkin' what woke me up. Now, Dusty was a one-man dog, you know, and he always slept on the floor next to Doc. But he was outside just a-barkin' and I knowed there was somethin' goin' on out at the corral. More coffee, Doc?"

"Not yet, sweet," Doc said, waving the steaming pot away.

"So, Doc got up and pulled on his britches and grabbed a rifle what was by the front door and walked outside in his stocking feet. I declare, it liked to scared me to death to hear them horses a-whinnyin' and Dusty barkin' like he'd treed a dozen coons."

"Mortenson don't want to hear all this, Ethyl. Why don't you look in on Sunny Lynn so's we can finish up with these papers?"

"No, that's all right, Mrs. Blaine," Mortenson said. "I want to hear the rest of the story."

Ethyl set the coffeepot back on the wood-burning stove atop the firebox and floated back to the table, a birdlike woman with her hair balled up in a thick bun at the back of her neck, her loose-fitting print dress hanging on her bony frame like a scarecrow's garb. Her sharp nose looked just like a bird's beak.

"Doc didn't catch the thief right then. When I come out, he was sittin' with Dusty and the boys were pouring out'n the bunkhouse like firemen runnin' for the fire wagon. That thief had got plumb away and killed Dusty with an old wagon axle, just beat that poor dog to death. Doc was squatted down, with Dusty's bloody head against his chest, cryin' his poor eyes out over that dog. He didn't care about the horses what the thief took, just that poor innocent dog."

"You didn't tell me the Mexican killed your dog, Doc," Mortenson said.

"I'm still broke up about it," Doc said.

"Doc set great store by that dog," Ethyl said.

Mortenson was touched. This was a side of the cattle rancher he had not expected to see. Most of the ones he had known over the years were a mercenary bunch without a trace of sentimentality. A dog was a dog, no more, no less. Mortenson wondered whether the Mexican had been hanged because he stole three horses from Blaine, or because he had brutally beaten a dog to death. One thing, sure. He wasn't going to ask such a touchy question.

"I think that's about got it, Doc," Mortenson said, showing him the final contract. "In bare-bones terms, you are to deliver three thousand head of white-faced Hereford cattle to the stockyards in Salina, Kansas, on or before June first of this year,

1879, whereupon, after inspection, ownership will transfer to one Mr. Albert Fenster, who will pay you the remainder of the money owed less that which I am advancing you today."

"I'm glad you cut out all that 'party of the first part' shit," Doc said. "Names is better. Mr. Blaine delivers to Mr. Fenster three thousand head of white-faced cattle for twelve dollars a head, and so on."

"There is a bonus of a dollar a head if you deliver by the first of June."

"Fair enough," Blaine said.

"I must also point out that should you not meet that delivery date, a deduction of fifty cents per day per head of cattle will be imposed."

"I notice your talk leans to the elegant side when you mention them rattlesnake clauses, like you just did."

"I just want to make sure you understand the exact terms of the contract, Mr. Blaine."

"And when you turn lawyer on me, I'm Mr. Blaine. In my day, we made deals with a handshake. Now we got to write every blamed thing down."

"That is the way of the world, I'm afraid, Mr. Blaine. Commerce has its own language, and before money changes hands, men draw up contracts to ensure satisfac-

17

tion and fair-dealing to all parties."

"Parties of the first and second parts," Blaine said.

"Exactly, Mr. Blaine. Now, if you will sign this contract, I will give you two hundred dollars to show Mr. Fenster's good faith."

"Fair enough," Blaine said again, and signed the contract.

"Now I will sign it and Mrs. Blaine will sign as witness. Fair enough, Doc?"

Blaine grinned to show that he now considered Mortenson an equal. After Ethyl signed the documents, Mortenson left them with a copy and stood up.

"I really must be on my way," he said. "Thank you both for your hospitality."

After Mortenson rode away, Ethyl sighed and looked sharply at her husband.

Doc folded the ten twenty-dollar bills and slid them into his pocket before he looked up at Ethyl, who stood there like some store clerk on guard against a potential shoplifter. There was a steely look on her face that told him she was about to offer not only an opinion, but an edict.

"Doc," she said, "you really ought to drive them cattle to Salina yourself."

"I know. But Sunny Lynn —"

"You think you can trust them two boys

18

to get along with each other on a long cattle drive?"

"Nope."

"Well, that's something I didn't expect to hear. So you don't trust them not to fight and maybe ruin us getting that money for our cattle."

"Neither boy is a-goin' to know that both of them are drivin' the cattle to Salina."

"How you aimin' to manage that?" she asked, suddenly not so stern of face, or critical in nature, but genuinely interested in what he had to say. "You goin' to lie to them boys?"

"Not lie, exactly. I just ain't goin' to tell either Jared or Miles that I'm makin' two separate drives. I'll send 'em different ways at different times. So it's likely they won't meet up until they both hit the stockyards in Salina."

"Then they'll get into it and likely try to kill each other."

"By then, it'll be too late, and I'll be there to pick up the money and give each boy his share. Which ought to make them both happy."

"So you are goin' to Salina?"

"I'll be there on the first of June, Ethyl. Them boys won't know they've been tricked till it's all said and done, wrapped up neat like one of your fried pies."

"You're takin' a mighty big chance, Doc."

"That's what life is about, Ethyl, takin' chances."

She snorted her disapproval of the lame homily and glared at him. Her light hazel eyes flashed green, and then yellow, just like the start of a prairie storm when the sky changes color, the clouds darken, and the sunlight breaks into shattered fragments that fade into an ominous dimness before clouds devour the light and blacken into charcoal.

"Life don't mean you got to lie to our boys, Delmer."

There she was again, using his given name as if she were scolding a child.

"I ain't lyin' to them boys, Ethyl. I just ain't tellin' neither of 'em the whole story."

"Hmmph. Deceit is the same as lyin'."

"I ain't goin' to split hairs with you, Ethyl. I'm just tryin' to make the best of what might become a bad deal if'n I do it any other way. You got to trust me."

"I trust you, Doc. I just don't trust them boys all that much. There's bad blood between 'em and it ain't goin' to go away."

"All over a damned woman," Doc said as he started for the door. He plucked his hat from the tree by the front entrance.

"Don't you go blamin' Caroline, now."

"I ain't blamin' nobody. I'll be back in a few days."

He walked out the door. Ethyl sagged. No goodbye hug, no kiss. That's just the way Doc was. When he had something to do, he went ahead and did it, and nothing got in his way.

She walked to the door and watched her husband ride off. He did not look back and she was glad she had thought to wrap some sandwiches and stuff them in his saddlebags while he and Mortenson were talking business. Doc probably knew she had done that for him. But she wasn't likely to get any thanks for her thoughtfulness. Doc wasn't insensitive. He just didn't believe in wasting words. He'd show his gratitude in other ways, she knew. He might buy her a pretty bauble or bring her a bouquet of wildflowers he had picked on his way back home. He wouldn't say anything, he'd just open her hand and put the gift in it and have himself a drink.

She loved Doc for what he was, not for what she sometimes wished he would be.

CHAPTER 3

Doc smelled the burning hair and hide a
few minutes before he rode up on the
branding corral, some two miles from his
ranch house. The odor floated on the stiff
breeze that still scoured the arroyos, rippled
the waters of the tanks, and made the grass
sway and flow like an emerald ocean. The
scent gave him a good feeling. He knew that
the gather was almost over and his calves
would all soon bear the brand of the Slash
B Ranch, increasing the size of his herd.

Tad Rankin, his foreman, raised a hand in
greeting as Doc rode up. He pulled the
branding iron away from the calf's left hip
and stuck it back into the fire, resting the
shaft on one of the stones in the fire ring.
Two hands, Joadie Lee Bostwick and Curly
Bob Naylor, released the branded calf and
watched it wobble off where two other
hands shooed it through the partially open
pole gate, where it cantered to its waiting

mother, tail wagging like a puppy dog's.

"Ho, Doc," Rankin called out. "You been getting any younger since I saw you this mornin'?"

" 'Bout as much as you got smarter since sunup, Tad. Give up the brandin' for a second, will you?"

Tad spoke to another hand nearby and walked over to the rails and climbed through. His lean body gave him plenty of room. He took off his heavy gloves and slapped them against his leg before tucking them in an empty back pocket. He spat out a stream of tobacco juice and shifted the wad in his mouth to the other side.

Doc dismounted and looped his reins around a pole, then started walking some distance from the corral. Tad walked beside him, knowing the boss was going to give him orders or chew his ass out for something.

"You got something on your mind, Doc?" Rankin asked.

"I'm gettin' together a drive to Salina over in Kansas Territory. But it's a little complicated."

"We ain't ready for no drive to Kansas right off, Doc. We're nigh to the end of the gather and I can't spare no men."

"Your men ain't a-goin', Tad."

"Pretty hard to make a drive 'thout'n no drovers."

"I'm makin' two drives, Tad. I mean, my sons are. Puttin' together three thousand head and five hundred of them will come from this herd. The biggest and the fattest."

"Oh, we can put five hundred head to pasture along the Canadian all right, and still have plenty to spare."

"We gotta move fast. I'm ridin' down to Dumas this evenin' to start Miles out and I want two hundred and fifty head driven down there come mornin'. Need to put trail brands on them afore you set out."

"Jesus Christ," Tad said. "We're still puttin' the Slash B on calves, Doc. Now I got to stop and trail-brand two hundred and fifty perfectly contented cattle and move them all the way down to Miles's spread. Hell, why can't he pick 'em up on his way out to Kansas?"

"Because I don't want him or his brother to know I'm sending two herds on the drive east."

"You got good reason to do such a tom-fool thing, I reckon."

"You know why, Tad."

Tad sucked in a deep breath that was like a penny whistle the way it sounded. He nodded.

Both Jared and Miles had fallen for the same woman, Caroline Vickers, back in school. She kept both boys guessing until they were all in their early twenties. Caroline was nineteen when she chose to marry Miles Blaine, who was twenty-one. Jared was twenty-three and thought he deserved to marry Caroline because he was the elder and had more land than either his father or Miles. He was furious and, before the wedding, which he refused to attend, he beat up Miles. It was a brutal fight, and when Doc broke it up, Jared vowed that he would someday get Caroline away from his brother.

"How you goin' to do that?" Ethyl had asked her son.

"I'm going to kill Miles and then Caroline will have to come to me."

"They'll throw you in prison, Jared. Maybe even hang you," Doc had said.

"Miles ain't gonna know what hit him and I sure as hell ain't goin' to tell. I won't be arrested for nothin' and I'll give the grievin' widder a home she can be proud of."

"You'd better not talk that way, Jared," his mother had said. "The Lord will strike you down if you even think about killin' your brother."

Yes, Rankin knew all about Caroline and

how she had kept both boys guessing until the last minute when she chose to marry Miles. That choice puzzled everyone, just about, until people began to look back and compare the two boys. Miles was easygoing and so adoring of Caroline, she could dominate him. He responded to her every whim. Jared, however, was aggressive, bossy, and demanded, instead of asked, for everything he wanted. And he wanted Caroline to worship him and obey his every command. People saw these traits in all three at church, pie socials, and dances. Jared was the jealous one and Caroline kept him dangling until she was staring spinsterhood in the face and chose Miles to be her husband.

"Tad, I'll expect those two hundred and fifty head in Dumas in two days."

"Three," Rankin said.

"Three, then, but I'll be back and you'd better have another two hundred and fifty head ready for the trip to Jared's up in Perryton."

"I can do that, Doc."

"I'm off, then. I expect you to carry out these tasks. As the contracts I signed said, 'Time is of the essence.' I got to deliver three thousand head to Salina by June first. If we beat that deadline, the price goes up a dollar or two."

"This time of year, I don't know," Rankin said. "Them rivers can be powerfully brutal. You might lose a few head and you might lose some time. And if them two boys meet up, you got a shit pile of trouble."

"Miles will start out first. He should get plenty of ground between him and Jared before Jared even leaves the barn."

"You hope."

"That's how I've got it figgered, Tad."

With that, Doc walked back to his horse with Tad and climbed into the saddle. He waved good-bye and rose off to the south, toward Dumas.

He knew Miles would come through and get together a herd. Jared might be harder to convince. They had all made a cattle drive or two, one to Wyoming, another to Colorado. They hadn't made much money and lost quite a few head on both those drives.

It wasn't Miles he was worried about as he rode across his spread toward the main road between Amarillo and Dumas. It was Caroline. She wanted Miles under her thumb and she'd fight him all the way as she had done in the past. When Miles was gone, she had no control over him and she was a jealous woman.

Buzzards flew in lazy circles in the sky. He

knew what they were eyeing and sniffing out. A wolf had gotten one of the yearling calves a few days before, and the scent of decomposing beef was still in the air. Nature held sway in the far reaches of his ranch and there was nothing he could do about it. In the past, he had fought off marauding Apaches, cattle rustlers, wolves, and mangy coyotes. The land wasn't the problem; it was ownership of the land that brought responsibility and guardianship. What he had must be protected. He looked on his ranch as a garden in olden times, like Eden. There were dangers lurking in every shadow, along every creek, and in every gully or arroyo. Men tended the land and its crops of hay and cattle, but he had to tend to his men. There were gray hairs for every challenge he had faced, every setback he had overcome.

As long as the Easterners demanded beef, he would thrive, he knew. Next year, he could put together his own large herd and drive them to the railhead. That would pay off his mortgage so he and Ethyl could finally enjoy the fruits of their labors. Then his garden would become another Eden and he would be its god.

CHAPTER 4

As Doc had expected, Miles wasn't at the ranch house when he rode up the following afternoon.

Caroline walked out onto the porch, the shadow of a frown on her still-beautiful face. She wore a green-and-gold gingham dress, with a green ribbon tied to her flowing straw locks of hair, dabs of rouge on her fair cheeks, and ribbons of rose lipstick on her full and pretty mouth. She looked as if she had just thrown on her dress. One side of the hem was higher than the other. And he also thought she had just tied her hair up with the green ribbon and hastily dabbed on her makeup. The dress was slightly wrinkled as well, as if she had just retrieved it from a clothes hamper.

"Well, howdy, Doc," she said, forcing a warmth that wasn't there. "What brings you down to these parts?"

She almost never called him Daddy or Pa

or Dad. He was always Doc to her except when she wanted something from him and Ethyl. It was something both he and Ethyl resented, but they had never spoken to Caroline about her lack of respect for her father-in-law. For that matter, she called Ethyl by her name, always. It was never Ma or Mother, as if both he and Ethyl were necessary evils, unwanted appendages to a man she wanted all to herself, without forebears or relatives.

"Came to talk to Miles, Caroline. Where can I find him?"

"What about?" she said, ignoring his question.

"Business."

"What business?"

"I'll let Miles tell you about it after I see him. Where can I find him?"

"Well, he's been at the gather for a week and I think he's branding the newborns."

"Can you give me some direction? North, south, east, or west?"

She was beginning to irritate him and he didn't want a fight with her before he talked to Miles. Nor afterward either, for that matter. He was tired and sore from the long ride to Dumas and he knew Miles would want him to spend the night. If there was any fighting to be done, it would be before, during, or after supper. Or maybe all three.

"Oh, all right," she said. "If you aren't going to tell me what you want to talk to Miles about so unexpected like this, he's probably at the north tank. It's a good stretch of the legs for you, Doc. Miles didn't come home last night because he's working so far from the house."

"It's a two-hour ride," Doc said. "I'll just water my horse and fill my canteen at your well, if that's all right?"

"Why, of course," she said. "You go right ahead, Doc."

She turned and left the porch, walked back inside the house. Doc didn't miss her at all. He rode to the well and dismounted. There was a water trough next to it, and he let his dun horse, Sandy, drink. He slipped the wooden canteen from his saddle horn and cranked the bucket down into the well. He heard the wooden pail splash when it hit the water. He jiggled the rope and heard the gurgle as the bucket sank and dipped into the water. He cranked the bucket back up and poured water into his canteen until it reached the top. He corked the canteen and poured the rest of the water into the trough.

Sandy slurped the water with its rubbery lips, dipping its muzzle in and out of the water, blowing and snuffling through its nostrils.

Doc felt that someone was watching him. He could almost feel a steady gaze on the back of his neck. Caroline? No reason for her to watch him. Unless she was anxious for him to leave. She probably was, but why? He walked around the trough until he had Sandy between him and the house. He peered over the horse's neck and saw a curtain move. The movement was very quick, as if someone had been standing at the window with the curtain open and then released the cloth.

Again, he thought, Caroline?

Why all the secrecy? She had every right to look out through the window. No need to conceal herself behind a curtain.

Doc pulled Sandy around and put a boot in the left stirrup. He hauled himself up into the saddle and started riding away from the house. He kept his gaze straight ahead until he topped a small rise, then bent down as if adjusting his boot in the stirrup and stole a sidelong glance at the house.

That's when he saw the back door open and a young man step outside. The man tucked in his shirttail and ambled off toward one of the outbuildings without glancing back at Doc. Doc straightened up and rode on. He knew who the man was, for he had sent him to his son a month ago, when Miles needed another hand for spring roundup.

The man's name was Earl Rawson. He was nineteen years old and hailed from Denver, or so he said. One thing for sure, he wasn't working cattle. And he'd bet that Miles didn't know that Caroline was cheating on him.

Maybe, Doc thought, his sons weren't the only two men Caroline had played with before she had married Miles. Maybe some of the stories about her had been true. Ethyl had believed them. He had not. But when it came to knowing what was in a woman's heart, he would have to defer to Ethyl. She had the instincts of a she-wolf when it came to predatory females. And Ethyl had never liked Caroline or trusted her. She hadn't wanted either of her sons to marry her.

"That woman has a mattress stuck to her back," Ethyl had said. "I wouldn't trust her as far as I could throw a wagon full of anvils."

What he had just seen might prove that Ethyl was right. Or maybe Earl had just carried a load of kindling inside the kitchen for Caroline's cookstove. Hell, he shouldn't jump to conclusions. Not now. Not when he had so much riding on Miles getting cattle to Salina. Maybe he would go so far as to tell his son that he should take Rawson on the drive. No use leaving a wolf in the henhouse while he was away.

There was the faint smell of sage and bluebonnets, the tang of lespedeza and alfalfa mixed with the scent of sweet clover as he approached the branding corrals. Carey Newgate was prodding a ganglylegged calf through the chute back to its mother, faint tendrils of smoke rising from the fresh brand on the dogie's hide. Miles was inside one of the corrals, pulling the branding iron from the cherry red coals while two other men held another calf down, one stretching out its hind legs, the other pinning down its neck while he had a choke hold that twisted the animal's neck. The calf's eyes were wide with fear, but it was pinned down by experts.

Doc sat his horse as Miles planted the iron on the calf's hip. There was a slight sizzle as the hot iron cooked flesh and burned hair, searing into the flesh a ROCKING M. He stepped away and shoved the branding iron deep into the coals while two men wrestled another calf out of the chute and splayed the kicking calf on the ground with brute force.

Miles looked up and saw his father sitting his horse.

"Hey, Pop, what brings you out here? How are you?"

"I'm just fine, Miles," Doc said, a sarcastic twang to his voice.

"Well, I can see that. Hell, is this a formal visit?"

"You got more mouth than sense, Miles. Crawl through the fence. I got business to chaw over with you."

"I'm always interested in business, Pop. How's Ma?"

"She's fair to middlin'," Doc said. "As usual."

Miles walked to the fence and climbed between the poles. "She's tough as a hickory knot, all right."

The two walked away from the other men who kept up the branding.

"What's on your mind, Pop? You find a buyer somewhere?"

"I did. That ad in the Salina *Register* got me a live one."

Miles dug out the makings from his shirt pocket, offered the sack of tobacco to his father, who shook his head. Miles slid out a paper and crimped it between his fingers, pulled the sack string, and poured an even line of tobacco into the trough. He licked one edge and rolled the paper tight, licked it again to seal it, and stuck the quirly into his mouth. Doc fished out a lucifer and struck it on his boot heel, held the match to the cigarette.

Miles drew a breath and sucked flame into the tobacco.

"Thanks, Pop," he said, and pulled the string tight around the sack. He slid papers and tobacco back into his shirt pocket and blew out a plume of purple smoke.

"Miles," Doc said, "the man in Salina wants upwards of fifteen hundred head at the railhead by June first. I'm running two hundred and fifty head down. Can you make the drive right away? I brought you a map. Should be easy."

"Kansas ain't easy, Pop."

"Easier than Colorado."

"Yeah, maybe. Fifteen hunnert head, eh? And you only got two hundred and fifty?"

"I want to make a little money. I can't get a big herd together just yet. That last drought dropped my numbers. But next year, by God . . ."

"Well, I can do 'er. Maybe a week to get that many ready for the drive."

"You ain't got a week, Miles. Two days at most."

Miles let out a long, low whistle.

"Jesus, Pop, we just finished the gather and I ain't sure I got all the newborns yet."

"You can tag the ones you missed when you get back. Way I figger it, if this man likes what he sees, he'll buy more, or word will get around that we got good cattle in the Panhandle."

"How much a head?"

"I quoted him twelve bucks. Could be a mite more, a dollar or two, if you beat the June deadline."

"So, maybe thirteen or fourteen dollars a head. Last I heard beef was bringing fifteen dollars a head in Abilene."

"Don't quibble, Miles. I already signed the contracts."

"I ain't quibblin'. Hell, it's more money than I've seen in many a moon. What about Jared? He know about this?"

"No. And I ain't gonna tell him. This is between you and me."

"Oh, I'm your favorite son now?"

"You always were, Miles."

"Pop, you lie like a Persian rug."

"Deal? I'll meet you in Salina on or before the first of June."

"Wished you were goin' with us, Pop. Yeah, I'll do her."

They walked back to the corral and Doc retrieved a map he had drawn, handed it to

Miles. "You stick to that route and you got plenty of grass and water."

"Anybody up there goin' to hit us up for tolls?"

"Not that I know of. Carry your rifles and pistols and act like you own the whole state of Kansas. You'll get through, I reckon."

"Still wished you was goin' with us, Pop."

"Just get them cattle to market, son. My small bunch should be here tomorrow."

"You take a lot for granted, Pop," Miles said, his face bright with a friendly smile. He was taller than his father, leaner, with brown eyes and brown hair. Sweat blackened his shirt and there were round patches under his armpits. He wore three days of stubble that made him look older than he was.

"You see Caroline?" Miles asked.

"We said hello. She told me where you was."

"Sweet woman," Miles said.

Doc said nothing. But he nodded and Miles did not see the cloudiness forming in his eyes.

"I got to go, son. See you in Salina."

"So long, Pop." He looked over at the chuck wagon parked some distance from the branding corrals. There was a lot to do. He crawled back through the fence and started talking to his men. He saw his father riding north and knew he would not look back.

Still, he wished Pop would be on the drive. Was he getting that old? And could he fill his father's boots?

It was a long way to Salina.

But Pop had told him something a long time ago that came to mind now.

"Experience is the best teacher," Pop had said.

Well, I guess it's time I went to class, Miles thought, and the grin returned to his face, much to the puzzlement of the men gathered around him. A calf bawled for its mother and one of the men stoked the fire with the business end of the branding iron.

CHAPTER 5

Freddie Morton did not hear the soft tread of footsteps approaching his bedroll. He heard nothing because he was fast asleep next to the branding corral, his face pale as pewter under the faint glow of starlight. He was the only hand there, since the others had ridden off to gather around 260 head of good beef stock and drive them to the Rocking M down in Dumas.

He jolted awake when he felt a strong palm slam over his mouth. He cried out, but his muffled voice soaked back into his throat like a sodden wad of cotton. He felt strong hands jerk him to his feet from atop his bedroll. He struggled, clawing for his belted knife, but his feet left the ground and he dangled between two strong burly men who smelled of onions, garlic, and the cloying fragrance of cilantro.

The men carried Freddie toward a live oak growing by Owl Creek. He saw another man standing over the mound of earth where they had buried the horse thief earlier that same day. He was holding a shovel and the tree cloaked him in deep shadow so that Freddie could not see his face.

Then he heard the liquid flow of Spanish issuing from the shadowed man with the shovel.

The other two answered him. Freddie did not understand even one word.

Then he was hurled to the ground. When he cried out in pain, one of the men who had carried him to that spot kicked him hard in his side, just below his rib cage.

"Levantase, cabrón," the shadow man spat.

"He tells you to get up," one of the other men said.

"Y callate," the shadow man said.

"He tells you to shut your mouth."

Freddie scrambled to his feet.

The man beneath the oak tree stepped toward him, holding the shovel like a warrior's lance.

But the man did not give the shovel to Freddie. Instead, he lifted something off his chest and dangled it before Freddie's wide eyes. Freddie saw that the object was a pair of old field glasses, binoculars that looked battered and worn even in the dim light of the stars and the pale ghost of a fingernail

41

of a moon.

"Do you know what these are?" the man said in heavily accented English. But he did not expect Freddie to answer.

"These are what we look through today and see you hit the horse. You make the horse jump away and the neck of our brother breaks from the rope around his neck."

"I — I . . . ," Freddie stammered.

Callate, tu hijo de mala leche," the man said, releasing the binoculars so that they thumped against his chest.

"Do you know the name of our little brother?" the man with the binoculars asked.

Freddie shook his head, too frightened to speak.

"His name was Manuel Gallegos."

"I — I didn't know," Freddie said. "They just said he stole some horses from Doc Blaine."

"Because his wife is very sick and she carried a baby in her belly. He wanted to take her to a doctor and he did not have any money."

Freddie shrank away from the man who was speaking to him, afraid to say anything.

"We follow Manuel to tell him it would do no good to steal the horses. His wife died after he told her that he would get money for her when he stole the horses."

"I — we — didn't know," Freddie said. "We just knew he —"

"You do not ask the questions, eh? You just bring the rope and take his life."

"No, no," Freddie said. "I didn't bring the rope. All I did was chase the horse out from under him. I was just followin' orders, honest."

"Where is the rope?"

"It's in the grave, I reckon. I think somebody just left it around his neck."

The man thrust the shovel at Freddie. Freddie grabbed the handle to keep from being knocked down.

"Dig," the man said. "You dig my brother out of the earth. And *ten cuidado*. You do not touch my brother with the blade."

Freddie began to dig. He started on the outer edge of the dirt mound and marked the boundary. Then he began to scoop dirt from the mound, paring it down until it was almost level. He dug around the edges, careful not to venture into the center where he knew the Gallegos body lay a-moldering. The three Mexicans watched him carefully. Freddie's hands began to shake and quiver, both from the strain of digging and from fear that the shovel blade would slice into

43

the dead man's body and perhaps chop off an arm, a hand, fingers, or even his head. Sweat beaded up in the furrows on his forehead and soaked his sleeves under his arms and dripped from his bony wrists.

Freddie was careful. He saw the dead man's trousers, his boots, his belt, and his shirt. He dug out dirt away from the body until it emerged on a platform of dirt, untouched. Dirt covered the dead man's face.

One of the brothers bent over and began to sob.

"*Pobre* Manuel," he wailed. Tears streamed from his eyes and drenched his face.

"*Calmate,* Jorge," one of the brothers said to him. "*No te lloras, mi hermano.*"

Jorge looked up at his brother, his face contorted with grief.

"*Se fue,* Carlos," Jorge said. "He is gone. Forever."

"*Sea un hombre,* Jorge," the man in the shadow said.

He took the shovel from Freddie and continued to look at Jorge. "*No muestra su cara a este gringo, esto pedazo de susio.*"

Jorge wiped his sleeve across his eyes.

"*Tenga razon,* Miguel," he said to his older brother.

"You are right. I must be a man. I must not show my face to this gringo. This piece of filth."

Miguel slapped Jorge on the back and smiled.

"We will bury our brother next to his wife, gringo," Miguel said. "We will bury you in this dirt here. That is where the worms will eat you. Your soul will go to hell."

"No, please," Freddie said. "I'm sorry. I'm sorry about your brother. Please don't kill me. I didn't want to hang your brother, honest."

Miguel reached down and picked up the piece of rope that was draped across his brother's body. He pulled the noose from around Manuel's neck after he loosened the knot. He held the rope up by the noose in front of Freddie's face.

"We will hang you, gringo. But you will not hang from a tree. You will die the slow death."

Freddie took a step backward. He looked at the rope in Miguel's hand as if it were a poisonous snake, a live snake.

Carlos jabbed the barrel of his pistol in the small of Freddie's back. Freddie stiffened and froze.

Miguel nodded to Carlos and Jorge, who grabbed Freddie's arms. Miguel slipped the noose over Freddie's head. He pulled the knot tight until it was snug under Freddie's ear.

"No, you will not hang from a tree like Manuel," Miguel said.

"Tie the gringo's hands behind his back, Carlos. Jorge, bring the horses. Quick, quick." All in Spanish, but Freddie knew what they were going to do.

He begged and pleaded with Miguel to let him live. He got down on his knees, but Miguel jerked him back up on his feet. He shook with fear and soiled his trousers. Miguel gave him a look of disgust as Jorge returned with their horses.

"I will drag you to death," Miguel said to Freddie. "You will strangle and die, but you will also scream to die."

Freddie was sobbing too hard to say anything. Carlos tied the end of the rope to his saddle horn. The brothers mounted their horses. All looked back at Freddie, who was standing there with his knees bent, his hands tied behind his back, his face soaked with tears. He was praying and crying when Miguel dropped his arm and the three rode off.

The rope behind Carlos's horse tautened and jerked Freddie off his feet. He pitched forward, his body slamming into the ground with a thud. Then he began to scream and the rope pulled his body along the ground. Rocks, stones, pebbles, and sand wore away Freddie's trousers at the knees, first, and then his shirt began to rip and tear. Sharp stones dug into his flesh. He screamed until Carlos spurred his horse to a faster gait.

Freddie's body rolled and bounced over the ground. His flesh opened up as Spanish bayonets and prickly pear spines gouged his skin and blood poured through dozens of open wounds.

Freddie screamed and screamed. Until he screamed no more and the Mexicans took one last turn to make sure Freddie was a corpse, then halted their horses by the open grave, where the body of Manuel still lay, his sightless eyes staring up at the stars.

In silence, all three Gallegos brothers lifted Manuel's body and threw Freddie's into the grave. They took turns throwing dirt on the dead man until he was no longer visible.

Carlos and Jorge walked a little ways from the creek and returned with a burro-drawn *carreta*. They lifted Manuel's body into the cart where they had laid out soft blankets. They did this with solemn reverence, while Miguel looked on with sad eyes.

"Let us go," he said. "Let us go home with

our dead brother."

"What about the others?" Jorge asked.

"We will get them," Miguel said. "We will get them all."

"We will steal their cattle, their horses, rape their women, and kill their babies," Jorge said. "Then I will be satisfied."

"I will never be satisfied," Carlos said. "Never."

Miguel said nothing. As they rode across the night lands, he tapped the binoculars dangling from his neck. The glasses knew who the others were who had hanged their brother. And so did he.

They would all pay, he vowed, for murdering their brother Manuel. He crossed himself and made the promise to God. Now, he thought, his vengeance would be sacred.

Somewhere along the creek, a coyote began to bay. Others joined in the chorus, until the air was filled with their yapping. They had discovered the fresh grave, the shallow grave, and were already beginning to scratch and dig. Tomorrow the buzzards would come, but tonight's feed belonged to the coyotes.

CHAPTER 6

Lenny Wexler rode the last loop of the night herd watch. His track took him close to the live oak by the creek near the branding corral. It took him within smelling distance of the Mexican horse thief's grave. He rode, also, very close to where a pack of coyotes were rooting like wild hogs in that grave.

"Hee yah, hee yah," Wexler yelled as he charged into the pack. He waved his hat and turned the horse in a tight circle as the coyotes retreated a few feet and formed a circle around the grave. The sun was just rising in the east, its fiery rim just above the creamy rent in the horizon. Clouds began to flow with colors as the sun painted their underbellies with salmon and gold. The sky was paling to a pastel blue and the morning star winked out, its silver swallowed up by the star closest to earth.

Wexler saw enough of the body to know, first of all, that it was not the horse thief

49

they had hanged the day before. He recognized the clothes and the part of the face that was still left. There was a rope around the neck of the dead man. Wexler gasped when he realized that it was Freddie. He felt a greasy swirl in his stomach and turned away to keep from vomiting. He swallowed air and gasped for a clean breath. He rode through the remaining coyotes and yelled at them. Somewhere on his circuit was another night rider, Jack Bledsoe. He rode into the opening maw of dawn, calling out his name.

Jack emerged from a shadowy clump of trees along the creek where several head of cattle were lined up, sucking water into their bellies. He heard the calls of birds in the trees and, behind him, the coyotes yapped in a ravenous chorus.

"Jack, Jack, come quick."

"What's up, Lenny? You seen a ghost?"

"Somebody killed Freddie and there's no sign of the Mexican."

"What?"

"Come see for yourself." Wexler turned his horse and galloped back toward the grave, Bledsoe right behind him.

A half hour later, Tad Rankin tried to make sense out of what he saw in the grave.

"Looks like they brung in a cart to haul the Messican off," said Norm Collins, one of the men going on the drive to Dumas. "Them small hoofprints probably belong to a burro."

"I agree," Rankin said. "No shovel left behind. Looks like they come prepared to dig up the man we hanged, and carted him off to someplace else."

Rankin shielded his eyes from the sun and gazed at the surrounding landscape. He made a full circle.

"Norm," Rankin said, "you're our best tracker. See that knoll way out yonder?"

Collins turned and looked in the direction Rankin pointed his finger.

"Yep," he said. "I see it."

"Just out of curiosity, ride on out there and take a look around. See if you can find any day-old horse tracks, like where men might have been able to see the hanging."

"I dunno," Collins said. "That's pretty far away."

"Do it," Rankin said.

Collins mounted his horse and rode out to the distant knoll. Rankin saw that he was staring at the ground as he rode. Collins could track an ant across a flat rock. He had been a hunter and guide down in the Palo Duro country until Doc had hired him when they were having trouble with Apaches a few years before.

51

"Anybody here know anything about this?" he asked the other men who had come with him after Bledsoe and Wexler had drawn them away from the work of rounding up the small herd for the drive to the Rocking M at Dumas.

One man spoke up, Pedro Coronado. "Do you know the name of the horse thief you hanged yesterday, Tad?"

"Nope. He was just a Mexican's all I know."

"I did not see him. I was not here," Coronado said. "But when I was in town last week, I heard talk of a man named Manuel Gallegos. I know one of his brothers, and he said Manuel's wife was pregnant and sick. She carried a baby and Manuel had no money to take her to see a doctor."

Tad swore under his breath. "Are you saying that Manuel stole those horses?"

Coronado shrugged. "I do not know. His brothers were in the cantina and they said Manuel was *'desperado.'* It could have been him."

"A hell of a note," Wexler said.

Collins returned from his study of the knoll and rode up to Rankin, who had just climbed back in his saddle.

"Anything?" Rankin asked.

"Boss, you got good instincts. Yep, there

was horse tracks aplenty round that little hill. And signs that three men dismounted, walked around. With a spyglass, they could see what was goin' on at that hanging tree, all right."

"Three men," Rankin mused, his gaze on the distant knoll.

"Manuel has three brothers," Coronado said. "They might have been following him after he stole the horses."

"I wonder why they didn't ride up and try to stop us from hanging their brother," Rankin said, turning his head to look at Coronado.

Coronado shrugged.

"Maybe they knew they was outnumbered," Wexler said.

"Likely," Bledsoe added.

"So, the Gallegos boys came back, dug up their brother's body, and then hanged poor old Freddie."

"They didn't hang him," Collins said. "They drug him. With that damned rope around his neck. Freddie must have screamed to high heaven."

"A horrible way to die," Wexler said, shuddering so that his upper torso shook.

"Slow and painful as hell," Bledsoe said.

"That probably means they ain't finished with us, boss," Collins said. "They got one of us and might just come after us, one by one."

"Well, we'll all have to be on our toes," Rankin said.

"I'll give orders to the other men and to Doc when we see him, to carry pistols and rifles and keep their eyes peeled."

"Good idea," Collins said, sliding a cut of tobacco into his mouth.

"Well, let's bury Freddie and get on with the gather," Rankin said. "And get that damned rope off his neck and burn it. It's already killed two men."

Some miles south of Amarillo, on the road to Dumas, Doc encountered them late in the afternoon. The wind was up and sand blew at the men, their horses, and the cattle.

"You're late, Tad," Doc said. "How come? I expected you to be further along."

"We had an incident," Rankin said. He told Doc about what they had discovered at the hanging tree and what he suspected might happen.

"I gave orders to all hands that they should carry weapons and be on the lookout for the Gallegos brothers. You'd better do the same."

"Good idea, Tad."

"You keep an eye out, Doc."

"I will," Doc said. "You tell Ethyl?"

"I did, and she put a rifle by the door and slipped a Smith and Wesson in her apron pocket."

Doc laughed, conjuring up the image of Ethyl arming herself.

The two men watched the cattle streaming past them. Both slipped bandannas over their faces to block the blowing dust.

"When you deliver these beeves to Miles, you send the other men back to the Slash B and you make the drive with Miles."

"You sure you won't need me?" Rankin asked.

"I need ten of you, Tad, but you're my rep. Miles might need you if he runs into any trouble."

"You expectin' any?"

"Nary a speck," Doc said with a sly smile flexing on his lips.

"See you in Salina, then, Doc."

"Try and beat that June first deadline, Tad. I'm counting on you."

"We'll do our best."

The two men parted company. Doc looked back once and saw that the small herd was moving along despite the wind and the streamers of dust blowing across the trail.

He had heard of the Gallegos family. They were poor farmers in the middle of cattle country. Their women wove blankets and made pottery that they sold in the outdoor market in Amarillo. He felt sorry for them, but a horse thief was a horse thief. Had Manuel Gallegos asked for money, he wouldn't have been able to give him much, but that was no excuse for stealing. And, in cattle country, you didn't steal a man's horses. There wasn't a man alive who didn't know that such an act meant the death penalty.

Death by hanging.

Still, he felt badly about the two dead men. Blood was on his hands and he did not know how to make amends.

The sun was setting by the time Doc rode up to the ranch house. Ethyl was waiting for him on the porch, a Winchester rifle close at hand, leaning against the wall next to the front door.

He could tell that she had been worried. What he dreaded was hearing her berate him for hanging Gallegos. She knew the law of the West, but she was against her husband seeking justice in such a way.

He was weary. He was hungry.

And he felt the weight of what he had done, despite his conviction that he had been right to hang the Gallegos boy for his felonious act.

"I don't want to hear it, Ethyl," he said as he wrapped his reins around the hitch rail.

"Well, you're going to hear it, Doc," she said. "In spades."

"I love you, darlin'," he said, trying to ease the situation before it erupted in his face. He smiled at her.

But Ethyl didn't smile back.

CHAPTER 7

Doc felt the cold morning wind bite into his bones. Dawn was just a weary pink scrawl on the horizon, as if the belly of a sockeye salmon had been ripped open with a skinning knife. Freshets of chilled air seeped through the button holes of his sheepskin jacket, and his face felt as if it had been sandpapered raw. His breath made little clouds of mist as if he had been breathing arctic air.

Roy Leeds, his *segundo,* rode with his left hand tucked under the armpit of his heavy jacket, his face beet-red, steamy breaths jetting from his rosy-rimmed nostrils in frosty plumes. Steam rose from the hides of the Herefords as they banged rib cages together into the teeth of the north wind.

"This is April, ain't it?" Leeds asked Doc without looking at him.

"Yep," Doc grunted.

"Seems more like December."

"Or January," Doc said. His teeth ground down the grit between them.

There were cattle strung out in a long line ahead of them as both men rode drag. They watched for strays or laggards as the bitter north wind whipped at them, lashed at their bodies and their senses.

"You picked a damned good time to run cattle up to Perryton," Leeds said, as if talk could lessen the chill that seeped into his bones.

"I didn't pick the time, Roy. The market called. I answered. Put it down to fate."

"Fate, my ass," Leeds said, his voice quavering as he fought the shivers. "More like the Devil."

"If you believe in such hogwash," Doc said. "Fate calls the turn in this life, Roy."

"Well, if so, she's a pure dee bitch."

Doc chuckled and the act seemed to warm him some, taking his own shivers to another level.

The small herd of about 270 head was approaching the Canadian River, on its second day on the trail. Roy and Doc rode drag, with two flankers, Randy Eckoff and Dale Walton, along with the lead man breaking trail, Jules Renaud, with his keen hawk eyes and with the instincts of a wolf. Jules would find the ford across the Canadian, and once across, they should reach Jared's Lazy J Ranch, south of Perryton, before nightfall.

The herd had not yet settled into a comfortable routine and Doc knew Jules had been fighting the leaders who kept wanting to turn back. The flankers kept the herd from breaking out of the caravan, but they had been taxed to the limit that first day. It should have been an easy drive, but its leaders kept changing as cows and steers fought each other for the top spot at the head of the herd.

"I can't see Jules," Roy said. "But I can sure smell river water."

"He's probably looking for a ford. You see Randy or Dale?"

"Yep. Some of the herd are trying to break ranks and get to the river."

"Well, they can handle it."

"At least we won't have to beat any of the herd back. By now they've all smelt water."

The herd picked up speed, their curly backs bobbing up and down as they trotted toward the river. The wind seemed to swirl and lash at them from different directions, but the brunt of it still came from the northwest, brutal and cold.

Doc closed the distance to the rear of the herd. He motioned for Roy to take the right flank, while he rode toward the left. He didn't expect any of the cattle to turn back on him, but they might bolt to catch up with those who were streaming off the flanks, leaderless and thirsty.

Doc looked ahead to see cattle streaking away from the herd in thick bunches. Then he heard Randy yell something.

A moment later, Dale hollered and this time Doc could hear what he said.

"They're cuttin', Randy."

Roy had his hands full suddenly, as the rear of the herd swung away, turning on him in a mad rush to escape whatever was chasing them.

Doc saw a man waving a horse blanket and chasing cows out of the herd. He was struck by the brazenness of the rider, rustling cattle in broad daylight in front of witnesses.

"You, there," Randy yelled. "Stop or I'll shoot."

Doc saw Randy pull his Winchester from its boot and put it to his shoulder.

A second or two later, he heard the sharp report of the rifle and then the whine of the bullet as it caromed off a rock several yards from the rustler. The rustler drew his pistol and fired over his shoulder at Randy.

Randy ducked but the shot was wild. He halted his horse and swung his rifle at the rustler. The cattle, responding to the gun-shots, stampeded in several different directions. Roy yelled out a curse and started chasing cattle that were breaking out of the right flank. He chased some of them back, but was soon surrounded by frightened whitefaces and his horse reared up and clawed the air with its front hooves.

By that time, Doc had to wheel Sandy out of the way of several head of cattle charging at him from two different directions. He too became encircled with cattle turning back toward him like mindless beasts with wide eyes and flashing hooves. He wheeled Sandy away from one bunch only to run headlong into another.

He knew it was hopeless to try and catch the cattle that had escaped the herd and were heading not only back toward Amarillo, but off to the east and west. Soon, he saw why.

There were two other riders cutting cattle out of the herd, driving them off in three separate bunches. He and his hands were almost outnumbered, he thought, even though they were five and he only saw three rustlers.

He rode down on one of them, who had just run off twenty-five or thirty head and was angling toward the west, his shirt flattened against his chest by the wind, his hat blown off and hanging by a thong between his shoulder blades.

The rustler saw Doc charging at him and drew his pistol.

Doc felt a sudden rage that boiled up from inside him and heated his face. He drew his pistol and made Sandy heel over in a tight turn with a tug of the reins. The rustler fired off a shot and Doc heard the bullet sizzle past him like a whirring hornet.

"Damn you," he yelled, and cocked his pistol as he raised it to eye level. The rustler stopped, whirled his horse in a tight turn, and fired from the hip when he was again facing Doc.

Doc lined up his sights on the Colt .45, held the front blade tight against the man's chest, and squeezed the trigger as he held his breath. The pistol roared and spat flame, sparks, and hot lead out of its black snout.

He saw the rustler stiffen and heard a smacking sound. Dust flew off the man's lined denim jacket and the rider grabbed his saddle horn and hung on as his horse continued to turn.

Cattle raced in all directions, spooked by these latest gunshots.

Doc heard more shots, from both pistols and rifles, and then he was next to the man he had shot.

"Who in hell are you?" Doc asked. He grabbed the reins of the man's horse and stopped it.

Blood bubbled up out of the man's mouth as he opened it.

"M-Miguel," he stammered.

Roy rode up a second later.

"I know who he is," he said. "That's one of the Gallegos brothers. You gut-shot him, Doc."

Miguel coughed and blood sprayed from his mouth, peppering both Doc and Roy with measlelike dots of crimson.

"Bastard," Miguel said. "You murdered . . ."

That was all he said. His eyes rolled in their sockets and he swayed in the saddle for a moment or two, then fell headfirst onto the ground. His legs kicked out and his body shook for what seemed an eternity to Doc but lasted only a few seconds.

"Looks like you put his lamp out, Doc," Roy said.

Doc gulped in a frosty breath of air and shoved his pistol back in its holster.

"Damn," he said, "I hated to do that."

"The man shot at you, Doc, and he was rustling cattle. We could have hung the son of a bitch and been within our rights."

"Killing men is not my idea of how to live life, Roy. We already killed his brother."

"Self-defense ain't no crime."

"Maybe not, but taking a life is a heavy burden for a man to carry all his life."

"You fought in the war, Doc. You killed men before this."

"Hell, he even looks like his brother," Doc said. "That boy we hanged."

"Bad seed. All of them Gallegos brothers. Look what they done here."

Doc looked around. He saw Jules ride up like a man who had just been robbed at gunpoint.

"They weren't rustling cattle," Doc said. "Those boys wanted revenge for their brother."

"Maybe we ought to hunt them other two down and just put their lamps out same as this one."

"That would be murder," Doc said. He looked at Jules and Roy. "But I'd sure as hell like to do just that."

"We got some rounding up to do, Roy," Jules said. "Ain't none of the herd crossed the river yet."

"We lose any cattle?" Doc asked.

"Hard to tell. But Randy and Dale run them other two off, so all's we got is a bunch of cattle roamin' free all over creation."

Doc sighed and slumped in the saddle for a long moment. Then he straightened up and looked at Jules with flint in his eyes.

"Then let's get to it, Jules. Let's round 'em all up."

"What about this one you laid out?" Jules asked.

"Let him rot for all I care," Doc said, and turned his horse to chase down cattle that were still running.

Jules and Roy exchanged glances.

"I reckon if we don't bury him," Jules said, "his brothers will find him and carry him back to Amarillo."

"Yeah," Roy said. "This'n they won't have to dig up."

The wind whipped at their clothes and turned their earlobes cherry red. It carried the heady scent of the Canadian River on its gelid breath and April no longer felt like spring in that part of Texas.

CHAPTER 8

Roy dismounted as Doc and Jules rode away. He walked over to the dead man and unbuckled his gun belt. He hung the pistol from his saddle horn and slipped Miguel Gallegos's rifle from its boot. It was an old Henry repeating rifle. The browned barrel was badly pitted, but the sights were sound and it was loaded. He poked the rifle inside his bedroll, then retied the thongs so that the bundle was tight. He mounted up and rode away, his head bent to shield his face from the wind.

He joined the others who were chasing down the stampeded cattle.

"Bunch 'em up," Doc shouted to Dale.

Dale turned three head of whitefaces back into a milling bunch of cattle that Randy was working back toward the remnants of the main herd. His horse bobbed and weaved under his expert control with his knees and the reins. Every time the cattle started to bolt, the horse charged and then stopped stiff-legged to block their progress.

"Randy's got him a good cuttin' horse," Jules said to Doc.

"You take that bunch and run 'em into the main herd, start 'em all back toward the river. We ain't got time to waste."

"Sure thing, boss," Jules said, and rode off. He too rode a splendid cutting horse. His horse danced into the same spot where Randy's horse had been as Randy turned his horse away and, spurred on by his rider, dashed off to go after strays that were farther away.

Doc rode off in a different direction. In the distance he saw a horse and rider galloping south toward Amarillo. He recognized the rider as one of those who had started the stampede. He stopped, pulled his rifle from its boot, and jacked a cartridge into the receiver. He put the rifle to his shoulder and took aim. By the time he lined up his sights, the rider had disappeared over the horizon.

"Next time, Gallegos," he muttered, and eased the hammer of his rifle down to half-cock and shoved it back in its boot. He spotted cattle settling down to a confused lope and chased after them.

"Go get 'em, Sandy," he said to his horse.

He eased up on the reins and gave Sandy his head. Soon he was herding cattle back toward the main herd, picking up strays on his way.

It was hard, grueling work, but Doc loved it. It took his mind off the icy winds that slashed at him with frozen razors of bristling air hurtling down at twenty to thirty miles an hour. He heard the men shouting to each other, and the wheeze of horses blowing mist from their nostrils as they worked the cattle back to the main herd. He ran in twelve head and shouted to Randy, who was returning with twice that number.

"Let's get a tally before we hit the river," he called.

Randy nodded and left Dale to keep the cattle in line. He rode to the head of the herd and started counting as he rode back to the rear.

After nearly an hour, Doc saw no more cattle out on the long, flat plain. He breathed hard and drew up at the rear of the herd, his chest burning as if he had inhaled fire.

"I counted two hundred and sixty-two head, Doc," Randy said. "Might have missed a few."

"Close enough. Likely any that we missed will turn up at another ranch or make their way back to the Slash B. I ain't gonna worry about it."

Roy rode up with three more head.

"Them boys weren't out to rustle cattle," he told Doc. "They was just tryin' to bust up the herd. But one of them boys shot two head before he lit a shuck back to Amarillo."

"Too bad we haven't got a chuck wagon with us," Doc said.

"I'd like to tack them two Gallegos brothers to a barn and set the barn on fire," Roy grumbled. "Bastards."

"Let's keep 'em movin'," Doc said.

Doc knew the river would be icy cold, but he knew Jules would prod the herd to cross it fast. He looked up at the sky and saw that the sun had cleared the horizon. Surely, he thought, the wind would abate and the sun would warm their chilled bones after they crossed the Canadian.

They forded the river at a shallow bend where it widened and felt the temperature rise as they headed for Jared's ranch south of Perryton.

The sun sent streamers of light and warmth across the trail, and the wind dropped off to feeble gusts that swirled around the men and the herd like mildly annoying breezes that had lost their feel of a late-winter gale.

When they rode onto Jared's land, late that same day, Doc told Jules and the others to bunch up the herd.

"Bed 'em down," he said. "I don't want them mixing in with Jared's cattle."

"Where?" Jules asked.

"Find a water hole," Doc said. "Turn 'em into a bunched-up circle with no place to go."

"You sound like you can read a cow's mind," Roy said with a grin.

"Them cattle don't have a mind to read. They'll follow any cow that will lead them."

"You got that right," Jules said. "We'll bed 'em down on some good grass near a tank."

"I'll ride on to the house and tell Jared my plans."

"Good luck," Jules said. "I just hope he's in a good mood."

"You let me worry about that, Jules," Doc said, and rode wide of the herd, which Jules had slowed to a crawl. Randy and Dale helped to bunch them up, with Roy closing the gap as drag rider. They hadn't lost a cow at the river crossing and Doc gave credit to Jules and Roy for that. A few cows had slid off the sandbars and gotten grabbed by the current, but Roy had chased them in the right direction and they had made the shore, cold and wet, but none the worse for their dunking.

One of Jared's riders spotted Doc and waved to him.

The two rode up on each other.

"You lookin' for Jared?" Bernie James asked Doc.

"Well, yes, Bernie, I am. He up at the house?"

"Not likely. He's with the vet up at the Sonoma section. Got him a case of pinkeye and he don't want it to spread."

"Shit," Doc said.

"Exactly. Jared's real worried. What's up anyway?"

"I'll let Jared tell you. But where's the main herd?"

"There's about two thousand head down by Rincon Creek. Rest of 'em's scattered all over creation."

Jared had named most sections of his large spread for easy identification. He used Spanish names because his foreman was an experienced Mexican cattleman named Francisco Villareal, whom they called Paco, because he didn't like the name "Cisco." Jared had enticed Paco away from the King Ranch down in the Rio Grande Valley by offering a higher wage and a percentage of profits. He had heard that Paco was a very savvy man with cattle, and his faith in the man had been proven out in the three years since he had hired Paco on as foreman of the Lazy J.

Jared was clinging to a corral fence when Doc rode up, a blind steer raking its horns at a spot where his son had been. Paco was yelling at the cow to draw it away from Jared while the veterinarian, holding his black medical bag, was on the outside of the pole corral looking in. Two more hands sat on the top rail, waiting to be called down to help bulldog the steer with the sightless pink eyes.

"Hi, Pop," Jared said, climbing to the top rail. "A little out of your territory, ain't you? Ma with you?"

"No, she's back to home. I got a business proposition for you."

"Light down and I'll give it a listen once we get some medicine in this damned cow's eyes."

"That the only one with the pinkeye?" Doc asked, as he ground-tied Sandy to a scrub of a bush near the corral.

"That's one too many," Jared said as Paco ran from the steer, which was hooking the air a couple of feet from Paco's butt. It tossed its head and snorted, pawed the ground, and then halted, its ears shaped into cones, twisting to pick up any sound from its imagined enemy.

Paco danced away on tiptoe and looked up at the two hands sitting on the top rail.

"Well, come on, boys," Paco said. "Get your thumbs out of your butts and hog-tie that steer before I lose my britches."

The two men, Al Corning and Chester Loomis, scrambled down into the small arena with dally ropes and approached the steer from behind on either side.

"Tackle him, Al," Chet said. "Grab his hind legs. I'll bulldog him."

"He's got shit all over his hind legs," Al said.

"Just lick it off once you get him down."

The steer turned on the two men. Chet grabbed the steer by the neck just behind its boss and wrestled with it. The steer kicked out at Al, who was trying to grab a hind leg, his little string of rope between his teeth.

The steer had diarrhea and was spewing urine and coffee-colored fecal matter from its hindquarters, splashing the smelly mixture onto Al's face and chest as he dived for the legs.

Chet wrestled the heavy steer to the ground. Al pounced on the hind legs and snapped the ankles together with one hand, while he wrapped the dally around both of them, knotted the rope, and pulled it tight. Chet grabbed the steer's horns and drove one into the ground and put his weight on the animal's neck to pin him to the ground.

"Okay, Doc," Jared said. "You can put that ointment in its eyes now."

The veterinarian, Abner Blassingame, set his bag on the ground, opened it, and took out a tube of medication. He unscrewed the cap as he climbed through the fence and stuck it in his pocket. He crabbed to the head of the steer and spoke to Chet.

"You got to hold him down real hard," he said.

"Do it quick, Doc," Chet said, and grunted as he put more pressure on the steer's head.

Blassingame grabbed an eyelid and squirted the thick yellow ointment into the steer's eyes. Then he opened the other eye and squeezed more of the tincture into its eye. The steer struggled to rise and Chet began to lose his grip.

"That should do it," the vet said. "Keep this one penned up and he should be okay in a few days."

He hurried out of the corral and recapped his tube of medicine and dropped it into his bag.

"That'll be six bits, Jared," he said.

Jared jumped down and dug into his pocket. He paid the vet and walked around to where his father was waiting.

Blassingame walked to his horse, tucked his bag into a saddle pouch, and rode off without a wave.

"Turn the steer loose," Jared said to Chet and Al, "then run like hell."

"Let's hope that's the only cow you got ailin'," Doc said to Jared.

"So far. What's this proposition you got?"

"I brought in about two hundred and sixty head from the Slash B," Doc said. "I want you to drive a thousand of yours to Salina, along with mine."

"That ad you put in the paper back there worked?"

"Like a charm. We get twelve bucks a head, a dollar more if you make it to the yards before June first."

"That's pushing it some."

"It shouldn't be hard. Could open up them Eastern markets for us."

"What about Miles?"

"Forget about Miles. This is between you and me, Jared."

Jared, who resembled his mother more than his father, with his sharp pinched face, thin lips, and stern, hawklike nose, stared at his father with coal black eyes narrowed to slits.

"I could maybe drive twice that number of good beeves to Salina," he said, suspicion clouding his eyes.

"That's all the man wants right now."

Jared wasn't stupid, Doc knew. If he suspected that Miles was also going to Salina, he would never agree to the drive. Doc tried to look as innocent and guileless as possible as his son scrutinized him with those dark eyes of his.

He felt like a man standing in the dock at court, waiting for Judge Jared to pass down his sentence.

CHAPTER 9

Jared Blaine walked to the nearby hitching post and unwrapped his reins. He led the cream-colored gelding he called Puddin' back to where his father still stood.

"Let's take a look at the stock you brought, Pa," he said. He glanced over at his father's horse. "I see Sandy don't look the worse for wear."

"He's just thawing out," Doc said. "We woke up to a blue norther this mornin'."

"It was fair and calm up here." Jared climbed into the saddle and waited for his father to mount Sandy.

Jared spoke to his men as he turned Puddin' in a circle.

"Make sure that steer don't get out," he said.

"You want us to stay here with it?" Chet asked.

"Draw straws," Jared said, and rode off to catch up with his father, who had already started to ride to the south where his herd was bedded down.

"So, you just want me to drive a thousand head to Salina along with your small bunch, eh, Pa?"

"That's right."

"Funny you didn't ask Miles. He's got more cattle than I do, I hear."

"Don't you worry about Miles none, Jared. Later on, maybe he'll make a drive."

"You always favored Miles."

"Not so, son."

"You sided with him with Caroline, when I wanted to marry her."

"I didn't side with him, Jared. It was plain to me and your ma that Caroline had made her mind up to marry Miles. Me and Ma just helped out with the wedding is all."

"She should have married me."

"Well, she didn't and that's that. You should be over that by now anyway."

"I ain't over it," Jared said, "and I ain't never goin' to be over it. One day, that woman will run off and leave Miles flat. She'll run right up to my ranch and we'll pick up where we left off. For good."

Doc didn't say anything. He could see that Jared's feelings ran deep and he was still carrying a burned-out torch for Caroline. If he only knew that Caroline wasn't the woman he thought she was, he might give up on that old worn-out dream. But he wasn't going to feed Jared's imagination by telling him that he suspected she was fooling around with one of Miles's hands behind his back. He might just ride down there to Dumas and try to get Caroline to run off with him. It was too damned bad that this woman had come between his two sons, for he cared for them both very dearly.

"You got a fine-lookin' bunch of cattle, Pa," Jared said as he looked over the herd. They were all bunched up, but not bedded down. They were gobbling grass like rabbits in the cabbage patch.

"It's about all I can rake up for this drive, but next year I ought to be able to put together a sizable herd."

"To drive to Salina?"

"If that market opens up to us."

"You're goin' to fill me in on the details, I reckon. Who the buyer is and all."

"Yes, but I'm going to meet you in Salina."

"You are?"

"Yes. I haven't met the buyer yet myself. I want to look over the situation and see if we can't make regular drives to the railhead every spring."

"I could do that for you, Pa."

"You could, sure. But I got the buyer. I

want to meet him face-to-face. Now I'm sending one of my men along with you. You have a choice."

"I could use an extra hand," Jared admitted. "I know a couple of these boys."

"You can have Jules or Roy. Take your pick."

Jared looked at the men who were circling the herd at various places, all walking their horses slow.

"Just one?" he asked.

"Just one, Jared."

"I reckon Roy, then. He's got a mite more experience than Jules. But they're both top-notch hands."

"They are. I think you made a wise choice. Roy knows Kansas and he's handy with a gun."

Jared jerked back in his saddle and stared at his father. "You expectin' we'll run into trouble? Gunplay?"

"Not particularly," Doc said. "We had some trouble down at the ranch a few days ago, and on the drive up here."

"How so?" Jared asked.

"I had to hang a horse thief," Doc said. "The man has, or had, three brothers, who want vengeance. They hit us south of here and I had to shoot one of them."

"Holy shit," Jared said. "And what about

the other two?"

"They run off, but I probably haven't seen the last of them."

"You think they'll try and stop us?"

"No, I don't think so. I reckon they'll stay pretty close to my ranch. They don't know anything about the drive you'll be makin'."

"A' course we don't know what we'll run up against in Kansas," Jared said. "We hear all kinds of tales from drovers who've been up there."

"I know," Doc said. "Rustlers, highwaymen, toll takers at roads and rivers."

"I reckon some of them tales is true," Jared said.

"You and your men had better pack plenty of iron, just in case."

Jared nodded.

"We will," he said.

Doc called out to Roy, who was coming toward them. Jules was riding in the opposite direction, while Dale and Randy were keeping an eye on cattle that kept straying from the herd and the water hole.

Roy rode up and touched a finger to the brim of his hat.

"Howdy, Jared," he said.

"How'd you like to go to Salina with Jared, Roy?"

"Why, I wouldn't mind. Ain't been there

in a while."

"I ain't never been there," Jared said. "How are the ladies?"

"Very kindly, mighty sweet, most of 'em," Roy said.

"Good whiskey too?"

"Good whiskey, and if you like the tables, they'll take your money same as in Dodge."

All three men laughed.

"We'll start the gather first thing in the morning," Jared said. "You know where the bunkhouse is."

"Seems like I remember it," Roy said.

"What about my cattle?" Doc asked. "Leave 'em here?"

"I'll get Paco to drive them up to where we'll take off. You and your men can stay the night if you like."

"I don't want to leave the ranch too long with your ma all by herself. We'll bunk on the trail back."

"You got that river to cross, Pa."

"I know. It was still wet when we left it a while back."

Jared laughed. "You know, Pa," he said, "you're still a tough old coot."

"I still got black hair on my chest if that's what you mean."

Jared slapped his father on the back. He looked at the western sky. "You say you run into a blue norther this mornin', Pa?"

"We turned blue in it," Roy said. "That's for sure."

"Well, look at that sky. Them winds didn't just come from nowhere. They's a storm building up out west sure as shootin'."

Roy and Doc saw the bulging elephantine clouds that were forming on the western horizon. They were turning black and the sun was gilding their edges as it sank toward the distant mountains, the Rockies, on its path to the Pacific Ocean and beyond.

"Will that stop you from leavin' in the mornin'?" Doc asked.

"It might. It will sure as hell swoll up the rivers if I read it right. Be a muddy start."

"I'd like to get that bonus money on our cattle," Doc said.

"Well, this is still April, Pa. We got better'n a month to make it to Salina."

"I'm countin' on it, son."

The two men shook hands.

"Roy, you come with me. Pa, I'll send Paco back with some hands to run your cattle in with mine. You tell Ma I said howdy, will you? I'll be sure and come down to see her when we get back from Salina."

"She'll be happy to see you, Jared. Good-bye." Doc paused. "And good luck."

"Will I be needin' it, you think?" Again,

Jared's piercing gaze with just a cloud of suspicion floating in his eyes like those swollen black thunderheads on the far horizon.

"We can always use a little luck in this life, Jared."

Jared's eyes slitted down tight and he turned away. He and Roy rode off to the north. Jules rode up then.

"So, Roy's going to make the drive," he said.

"Yeah. Any objection?"

"Nope. I was hopin' to run a sizable herd up to the railhead one day, though."

"You will, Jules. Maybe next spring."

"I gather we're headin' back pretty quick."

"No use dawdlin'," Doc said.

"See them black clouds yonder, Doc?"

"Yeah, there's a whale of a storm a-comin'."

"More cold winds. We're liable to be caught out in the open right in the middle of it."

"Likely."

"We could bunk up at Jared's for the night."

"I got to get back home, Jules. I don't like Ethyl bein' by herself with them two Gallegos boys on the loose."

"They wouldn't hurt no woman," Jules said. When Doc just glared at him, Jules

85

said: "Would they?"

"I just don't know what them boys would do. They might have no sense, seein' as two of their brothers are dead. Both at my hands. They might want blood for blood."

"Serious?"

"Real serious," Doc said, and looked again at the sky. He shivered involuntarily. He could almost feel the cold and the wet that was to come. There was an angry sky to the west, and from the looks of the clouds, they were floating toward them. If they could cross the Canadian before nightfall, they might find someplace high and dry to spend the night.

From experience he knew they could not seek shelter in an arroyo or a ravine. Many a cowman had died in flash floods that ravaged Texas during the heavy rains. It was spring and those rains could be frog stranglers, he knew. Yes, they could bunk the night at Jared's, but it was one more night away from his home and he was concerned, if not worried, about Ethyl. Oh, he had good men still at the ranch, but with a couple of hotheaded Mexicans bent on revenge, there was no telling what they would do.

He had made up his mind. They would head back home right away.

He just hoped the storm was slow-moving

and would stay north of them long after nightfall.

The sun disappeared behind a new phalanx of black thunderheads and they seemed to grow larger as he waited for Paco and his men to come for his herd. He could almost smell rain and a moment later, the breeze quickened and splashed against his face.

The soft wind carried whispers of rain in its throat and its fingers were already turning cold when Jules and three cowhands appeared on the horizon, heading their way.

Doc raised a hand in greeting.

"Get ready, boys," he hollered to Dale and Randy. "We're headin' for home in two shakes of a lamb's tail."

They didn't answer, but looked at Doc with crestfallen faces.

Jules snorted.

"They don't like leavin' any more'n I do," he said.

Doc said nothing. He didn't want an argument or mutiny from his men. Let them grumble and moan. They all had slickers and had already weathered a cold morning. One more night or two on the trail wouldn't kill them. And he was, as Jared had said, still a tough old coot.

CHAPTER 10

Miles soaked in the wooden tub on his back porch. Caroline kept adding scalding hot water to the soapy mix, as her husband immersed himself in the suds, his head lolled back, the stub of an unlit cigar in his mouth. He didn't notice how blanched her face was, nor how nervously she trotted back and forth from the kitchen with the steam kettle.

"That's enough hot water," he told her when she poured the sixth pot into the tub.

"I should think so, Miles. You've been soaking for more than a half hour. Probably scrubbed yourself raw."

"Oh, I'm clean as a whistle," he said. "It's my muscles that needed the hot water."

"Feel better now?" she said, without really caring how he felt.

"Some."

"You're leaving early in the morning for Kansas?" she asked.

"Before sunup. Herd's all gathered and

bedded down. Nearly two thousand head of whitefaces, well, about eighteen hundred head, more or less."

"Don't wake me up when you go," she said, handing him a towel as he stood up, his body covered with soap bubbles. She turned away to keep from looking at his nakedness and held the bath towel at arm's length.

Miles took the towel and stepped out of the tub onto a small Mexican throw rug of rope woven into ovals. He dripped soapy water onto the manila rug as Caroline stepped away and stood in the doorway, looking out beyond the porch at the pump and the water trough some yards away from the house. The sky was a velvet black, littered with billions of sparkling stars. Fireflies streaked over the empty field, winking off and on like tiny golden suns.

"Your clothes are on the chair," she said, and left the porch.

Miles hummed as he dried himself with the towel. The song was "Oh! Susanna," and he was slightly off-key. He could hear Caroline banging pots in the kitchen and his stomach roiled with hunger. It had been a long, hard day rounding up better than fifteen hundred head of cattle, while some of the hands marked them with trail brands for the drive to Salina. He used the same brand as his father had, since they were all going to be part of a single herd. The roundup had gone smoothly because he had good hands. They left out the mothers with young calves, the yearlings, and the two-year-olds. He was satisfied that they had good fat beef stock to drive to the railhead in Kansas.

Caroline had set the table and when he sat down, she brought in platters of beef and a bowl of mashed potatoes, a porcelain tureen of gravy and warm glasses of tea. Then she set a boat of greens near his plate. He tucked a napkin over his shirt and picked up his knife and fork.

"I'll get a ladle for the gravy," she said, and left the room while he piled food on his plate.

When she returned, he had spooned a crater in his potatoes. She handed him the ladle and he poured gravy into the depression. Caroline sat down and tied a large napkin around her neck. The lamp in the center of the table flickered with yellow light and the table danced with swimming shadows that slid around like scraps of black felt or floating bat wings.

"You don't want to see me off, Caroline? This is kind of a historic drive up to Kansas.

For me anyway."

"I don't want to look at a bunch of smelly cows dropping their pies and clumps of offal while you ride off into the sunrise," she said.

"Them cows is our livelihood, honey."

"Oooh," she exclaimed, "pardon me. They might mean money to you, but to me they're just a stinky bunch of dumb cattle leaving smelling plops all over the ground."

"You knew I was a cowman when you married me," he said as he forked a chunk of steak into his mouth.

"I knew you raised cattle, but I thought you had men to work for you. Sometimes when you come in at night, you reek of cow dung."

"That's money you smell, darling. Greenbacks on the hoof."

"I just didn't know anything about cattle ranching, Miles. I have to drown myself in perfume so I won't smell what you bring into the house."

"I'm sorry you feel that way, darlin'."

"You know how I feel?" She laughed ironically. "You haven't the least idea."

"Maybe you ought to get to know our cows better," he said. He masticated the beef into pulp, but did not see the fierce glare in Caroline's blue eyes. They were in shadow, as she intended them to be.

Caroline picked at her food as if she were preoccupied with other thoughts. She was. She took dainty bites and seemed to be forming unspoken words in between swallows of meat and potatoes.

"When you get back with some money, Miles," she said, "maybe I can get a maid to help me with the chores."

"We never had a maid," he said.

"When are you going to finish that extra room? The house is too small and the back porch needs to have a screen on it. Some evenings the mosquitoes eat me alive."

"I can't spare nobody right now to finish off that room." They lived in a small frame house that Miles envisioned would grow as their fortunes increased. The extra room was framed in and on a solid foundation, but it had no walls and only part of a roof. He had done most of the work himself on those late afternoons when he had come home early.

"Who all are you taking with you to Kansas?" she asked, finally, as she finished eating and sat there sipping her tea.

"Pa left me Tad Rankin, who's going to be trail boss. And I'll take Joadie Lee and Curly Bob and that kid from Denver, Earl Dawson. I'll probably need Carey Newgate to ride drag."

"You're taking Earl Dawson?"

"Yep. He needs the experience."

"But I could use him around here. He was helping me with that lintel over the front door and he said he could work on that extra room while you're gone."

Miles looked up at her, but Caroline leaned back in her chair so that her face was in shadow, just above the circle of lamplight. "When was Earl fixin' that lintel?"

"Today. For a little while."

"He was supposed to be working the gather."

"He just happened by and I asked him if he could fix it," she said.

"Well, you don't do no more of that. Earl's a cowhand, not a carpenter."

"He did a pretty good job."

"I didn't know the lintel was broke."

"You never know anything about this house or what I do all day, Miles."

"You got your work and I got mine."

She untied her napkin and threw it down on her plate. She rose from her chair. The legs scraped on the hardwood floor with a wrenching squeak. "I got too much work, what with the dust and the wind and the cows to milk, the hogs to slop. I need a maid and you're too cheap to get me one."

Miles looked up from his plate. He was almost finished eating, but Caroline's tirade caught him by surprise.

"You ain't complained before now," he said. "Now you need a carpenter and a maid. What else?"

"I need a husband with regular hours, Miles. Sometimes you don't get home until after midnight and sometimes you camp out with your men and I don't know if you're alive or dead."

She was about to break into tears. Miles scraped his plate, took one last dollop of potatoes and gravy, washed it down with tea, and stood up, his napkin stained and dripping from his collar like a bib.

"Damn it, Caroline, you pick the damnedest time to raise a ruckus about what I do and how overworked you are. I'll be gone for better'n a month on this drive and you got to blow your stack at me the night before I leave."

She glared at him. "Most of the time you're too tired to talk to me when you come home. Especially during spring roundup."

"I talk," he said with a stubborn tone in his voice.

"You talk about cows and coyotes."

"What about in our bed?" he asked. "I

ain't talkin' about cows then."

"No," she said. "You hardly talk at all."

"What in hell does that mean?" His ire rose in him as her own voice grew to a shrill pitch.

"I just hear you grunt and moan and when you're finished you turn over and go to sleep. Leaving me unsatisfied."

"Unsatisfied? What are you, a damned harlot? Ain't once a night enough for you?" He started toward her, but she backed away.

Then her voice softened. "Not always. Sometimes you go off and leave me behind," she said.

"Huh?"

"You satisfy yourself. Not me."

"Well, I don't know how I can do more'n what I do with you. I give you all I got."

She bit her lip.

She wanted to tell him that sometimes she yearned for more, especially afterward. She wanted him to hold her and cuddle her, but he was often too tired to do more than service himself and then fall asleep. She didn't say it then, though, and it was just another thing she kept to herself.

Like so many other little things that annoyed her about her husband.

"All right," she said. "I'm too tired myself tonight to argue with you. I just want a little consideration now and then, is all."

He walked to her and put a hand on her hair. He stroked the strands and looked at her as if she were a child.

"I'm sorry, darlin'," he said. "I'll try harder to please you. When I get back from this drive, things will be different. A lot different."

"Promise?" she said, and stretched her neck to kiss him.

"I promise," he said. He kissed her and then broke away with a sigh.

"What's the matter?" she said.

"We'd better not get started, Caroline. I got a lot to do in the mornin' and . . ."

She drew in several deep breaths. Her eyes were smoldering with repressed anger.

"Leave Earl here," she said as he walked toward the bedroom. He unbuttoned his shirt as he walked out of the small dining room.

"All right," he said as he turned into their bedroom.

The minute he said it he wondered if he wasn't making a mistake. Earl was a good cowman and showed much promise. If he could help Caroline and do some of the work for her, well, he could spare him. But at the back shelf of his mind was the nagging thought that something was not quite right about her request.

He just couldn't put his finger on it right at that moment.

Besides, he was eager to get the herd moving in the morning. He relished the thought of taking cattle across new country and to a new town. He wanted the money, but he also wanted to make his father proud of him. He was so excited he was ready to whoop and holler, but he was also very tired and knew it was going to be hard as hell to get up before dawn, saddle up, and join his men before the sun even cleared the horizon.

He fell asleep as soon as he stretched out on the bed and pulled the coverlet over him.

Outside, a pack of coyotes chorused in the distance, but he never heard them. Caroline sat up for a long time after she washed and dried the dishes and put all the food away.

She smiled to herself while she sat in her chair in the front room, moonlight drenching the front porch and staining the grass with a dull silver sheen. It was peaceful there and tomorrow Miles would be gone for more than a month.

And she would have Earl Dawson to share her bed with no one the wiser.

Chapter 11

Jorge Gallegos had no more tears for his dead brother Miguel. He and Carlos had been riding back to Amarillo for two long days and a night. The body had begun to ripen immediately after they found him lying next to his grieving horse, stripped of his gun belt, his rifle missing. Carlos was inconsolable and was still sniffling when they approached the adobe dwelling where they lived with their mother, Esperanza, on sixteen hectares of land on the eastern outskirts of town.

"You go and tell Mama we bring Miguel home to lie with our father and brother," Jorge said, in Spanish.

"She will cry."

"We will all cry until Miguel is under the earth. Go."

"What do I say to our sister?" Carlos asked.

"Tell Perla to help Mama wash our brother's body with soap and water. I will begin to dig the grave."

"*Ay de mi,*" Carlos exclaimed. "I wish to die before our mother and sister see our dead brother."

"You will die soon enough, Carlos. *Vete. Andale.*"

Carlos put the spurs to his horse's flanks and raced off. The long Spanish rowels dug into the soft spots just in front of the horse's haunches and it galloped toward the adobe, its whitewashed walls blushing pink in the early-morning sun.

Jorge headed toward the small cemetery where his father and brother lay under mounds of dirt, their graves marked by wooden crosses bearing their names and dates of death. He could not say why he rode there, except maybe to examine the earth before he got a shovel and began to dig six feet into the ground when the sun would beat down on him and his body would run with sweat.

He heard his mother's screams as he pulled up in front of the two graves. A moment later, he heard his sister wail and the two sounds mingled into a high-pitched screech of anguish. He turned his horse and plodded toward the house with its flower beds surrounding it and saw his mother tearing at her hair and pulling on her dress as if to rip them both off in a visual demonstration of grief. Perla, barely sixteen, began to scream at the top of her voice and jump up and down as if to hurl herself to the heavens or plunge herself into hell.

"I am so sorry, Mama," Jorge said as he rode up.

"Is he dead?" his mother demanded. "Is Miguel dead?"

"Yes, Mama, he is dead," Jorge said.

Carlos dismounted and hugged his sister, holding her tight to his chest.

"Oh my God," Esperanza cried, "my God, why did you take my son?"

"Perla," Jorge said as he stepped down out of the saddle, "boil the water and clear the table. I will carry Miguel inside so that you can wash him. I will take off his clothing."

"Let me see him, let me see him," Esperanza shouted, rushing toward Jorge's horse.

Jorge stepped into her path and stopped her. Miguel's body was draped over his old saddle, facedown, and Jorge did not want her to see the hole in his torso, the dried blood around the wound. But he knew she could smell him. They all could smell him. His mother knew Miguel was dead, but she could not force herself to believe it.

"Mama," Jorge said in a soothing voice,

"go into the house and help Perla. I will carry Miguel into the kitchen and you will see him."

His mother screamed and pounded fists into her cheeks as Jorge turned her around and pushed her toward the house. She was bent over, weeping, and walking with a stiffness that made it seem as if her legs had turned leaden. He watched as she disappeared inside and then turned to untie Miguel and carry his body into the house.

His mother screamed when she saw the dried blood and the bullet hole.

"What happened?" she cried. "Who did this to Miguel?"

"Carlos will tell you, Mama," Jorge said. "I go to dig the grave."

"Get the priest," his mother demanded. "Perla, go and get Padre Delgado. Bring him here. Miguel must have the last rites. Go quickly."

Perla stumbled away from the stove and ran out of the house. It was a short distance to the mission church and she ran like the wind as Jorge began to remove his brother's clothing as he lay, his eyes closed, atop the kitchen table. He let the clothes fall into a heap, which his mother snapped up and hugged to her face as she breathed in the horrible scents clinging to the fibers.

"Carlos, you help our mother while I dig his grave."

"I will help her," Carlos said, dazed by both the sight of his naked brother's body on the table and his mother's sobbing into his brother's clothes before she set them on the sideboard next to the sink.

When he had finished taking off his brother's boots, Jorge stepped outside, walked to the lean-to shed, and took one of the shovels in hand.

Perla returned shortly, Padre Ernesto Delgado in tow, his cassock flapping as he tried to keep up with her. He carried a small satchel in one hand and a breviary in the other, his tricornered hat askew on his head. Streaks of gray hair streamed over a shiny bald spot.

Jorge stopped digging and returned to the house to watch as Padre Delgado administered extreme unction. He and Carlos removed their hats and stood by with Perla and their mother in reverent silence as the priest intoned the Latin words. By then, Miguel's body had been washed and his hair combed, still barefoot, but garbed in a clean freshly ironed shirt and clean trousers. Perla sobbed quietly as she leaned against Carlos, who had an arm around her. Jorge embraced his mother, who crossed herself and muttered a voiceless prayer as she looked down at her son's dead face. Miguel looked as if he were asleep, but his skin was already darkening and his chest did not heave with breath.

Padre Delgado made the sign of the cross on Miguel's forehead and Jorge heard him say, in Latin, *"In nomine patre, et filio, et spiritu sanctu,"* as he bent over his brother in what seemed to be a final farewell.

"May God have mercy on his soul," Padre Delgado said in Spanish as he stepped away from the table.

"Will you say words over him when we place him in his grave?" Esperanza said to Delgado.

"I will do that."

"Come with me, Carlos," Jorge said. "We will finish digging the grave of our brother."

Carlos got another shovel from the lean-to and the two men finished digging around midmorning when the sun was high and beating down on their sweating bodies. They left the shovels and walked back to the house.

"We are ready," he told Delgado and his mother. Perla was in one of the bedrooms, still sobbing in disbelief that another of her brothers was dead.

"Vengeance is mine, sayeth the Lord,"

Padre Delgado reminded the small assemblage in his short funeral oration. He spoke in Spanish, and they all knew that phrase from the Bible. He reached down and picked up a handful of dirt and let it trickle from his fingers onto the blanket-wrapped body of Miguel. "Ashes to ashes, and dust to dust . . . ," he said, and at the end, made the sign of the cross over the grave.

"I am so sorry, Esperanza," he said. "God will give you the strength you need to overcome your grief."

"Thank you, Padre," Esperanza said.

Her sons began to shovel dirt onto the corpse. The dirt hit the blanket with soft swishing sounds until both Perla and her mother turned away and consoled each other as they both began to weep.

"I will say the rosary for Miguel," Esperanza said. "And I will make lunch for us. Come inside when you have finished and put your horses away."

"Yes, Mama," both men said in unison, and continued to fill up the grave, their shirts plastered to their bodies with boiling salty sweat.

At lunch, Jorge told his mother how Miguel came to be shot and killed. He told her of how he, Miguel, and Carlos had scattered

Doc Blaine's cattle and Carlos said he had shot two of them when he was riding away.

"When we did not see Miguel, we went back and found him," Jorge said.

"Do you know who shot him?"

"I think it was Blaine. But I was a long way from where it happened, so I could not tell for sure."

"He must pay," Esperanza said. "The old man Blaine must pay for what he has done."

"We do not know where he is, Mama," Carlos said. "We think he was taking the cattle to the ranch of his son. Maybe to Perryton."

"He will return," Esperanza said. "You must take away from him what is most precious to him. Just as he took the lives of two of my sons."

"We do not know what is most precious to him," Carlos said.

"Perhaps his own sons," his mother said.

"One of the sons, the one called Miles, he has a wife," Jorge said.

"Ah, he can get another wife. You must make the old man Blaine pay. He is the one who must pay."

"How?" Jorge asked.

She looked at both sons and reached across the table. She placed one hand on Jorge's hand and the other on Carlos's hand. She smiled wanly.

"That you must decide for yourself," she said. "You will know when the time comes. You will know."

"What about what the padre said?" Carlos asked as his mother took her hands away. "About vengeance."

"Ah, the vengeance," she said. "And how does the Lord work? He works through His people, through you and me. It is the Lord's vengeance, but you must be His hand on this earth, in this life. You must do the work of the Lord, my sons. He will bless you and I will be grateful if you do this."

"We will do it, Mama," Jorge said. "We will make the old man, Blaine, pay for what he has done."

"Tomorrow," she said, "you will get a cross and have the sign painter put the name of Miguel on it."

"To be sure, Mama," Jorge said. "Tomorrow."

They all visited the grave that night and said silent prayers for Miguel. They held hands under the stars and embraced each other. They were sad, but they drew strength from each other and that night Carlos, Jorge, and Perla all heard their mother saying a rosary for their brother. They crossed themselves and went to bed, there to sleep and dream of what they had lost and wonder at the mystery of life itself.

Chapter 12

Tad Rankin, trail boss for the Rocking M on the drive to Salina, had a gut feeling that started soon after he got the herd moving off Miles Blaine's ranch.

Trouble, to Tad, was a Hydra-headed temptress just waiting to pounce on the unsuspected.

He didn't voice his concerns to Miles, since he knew they were premature, and they might show him to be weak. But from the outset, he knew he was dealing with green hands and a boss, Miles, who, in his estimation, was not capable of planning a drive of this size. Miles had taken cattle up to Colorado, he knew, but had no part in the generalship of that drive. As far as Tad was concerned, Miles was just another greenhorn cowhand.

But he was going to treat his boss with respect and allow Miles to believe that he was in charge. That last feat would add to his worries, but Tad was accustomed to responsibility. That was why Doc had made him trail boss, he knew.

"Do we have enough hands, Tad?" Miles asked once the herd was moving north. "I had to replace Earl Rawson with Rudy Manley. Rudy's only eighteen, a year younger than Earl."

"As long as Rudy follows orders, he'll be okay. Better'n that Rawson you left behind."

"Oh, you didn't like Earl?"

"That boy's a slacker. His mind is on something else besides cattle. I seen that right off."

"I thought he was a pretty good hand," Miles said. He and Rankin rode drag while Joadie Lee and Curly Bob were trying to sort out the confusion at the head of the herd, with cattle vying for the lead, fighting for top spot.

"He sure didn't have no yen for this drive," Tad said.

"He told you that?"

"Not in so many words. I asked him a few questions yesterday afternoon and I just didn't like his answers."

"You read men pretty good, do you?"

"I reckon so. That's what Doc, your pa, tells me anyway. That's why he made me foreman of the Slash B."

Some of the cattle began to stray from the middle of the herd. Tad saw that Rudy was having trouble.

"You stay here while I ride up and get them cows back into the pack," Tad said, racing off to help the new man, Rudy.

Miles watched in fascination as Tad deftly guided his horse straight at the leader of the rebellion, turned him back into the herd, then whipped his horse in a tight circle to bluff the others back in line. He did it all in a few seconds while Rudy scratched his head in bewilderment.

Tad spoke to Rudy, but Miles couldn't hear what he said. Moments later, though, Rudy was yelling at the cattle and slapping his thigh as he rode alongside the left flank, as if to establish dominance over that part of the herd.

"Nicely done," Miles said when Tad returned to ride alongside him. "What did you tell Rudy?"

"I told him he had to show the herd who was boss. The kid'll be all right. Let's check that right flank, just to be sure we don't have no strays bolting for home."

The two men rode to the other side and watched as Pedro Coronado drove a lone deserter back into line, using his horse to block the cow every time it took a new track and, finally, driving it back into the herd until it was just one more animal among many, without a will of its own.

"We've got to turn this herd into a single body," Tad said. "We want all the cattle to play follow the leader. The trick is to keep them tight bunched, but give them room to walk without bumping into each other's butts. Once they get into that routine, they'll follow the leader over a cliff."

As if to illustrate his words, Tad rode up on the rear and yelled, "Hiya, hiya," at the stragglers and nudged them closer to the pack. The other cattle in front of them closed ranks and bunched up until they found tracks for themselves.

"You do that well, Tad. Like Pa. He knew how to keep a herd rolling along."

"Yep, your pa is plenty savvy about cattle."

They bedded down the herd that night, after making about fifteen miles. The chuck wagon caught up to them at sundown, with Carey Newgate, the cook. Tad had chosen him because he not only could cook, but was a good hand with cattle. Grumpy old Lonnie "Skeeter" Parsons, the regular cookie, had been left behind, much to his displeasure.

"Skeeter," Tad had told him, "you got the rheumatiz and a bad stomach from eatin' your own grub. 'Sides, the onliest thing you know about cattle is how to butcher 'em."

"You'll be sorry, Tad Rankin," Skeeter had said. "Once you taste Newgate's vittles, you'll wish I was the cook."

"If I have to, Skeeter, I'll send a man back to fetch you and save us all from starvation."

Skeeter fumed the whole time that he was helping Carey stock the chuck wagon, and was still moaning when they pulled out with the herd, leaving him behind.

The wind howled during the night, but dropped off before morning. Tad had the herd rolling before dawn after an early breakfast of beef, biscuits, thick gravy, peaches from airtights, scalding strong coffee, and bear claws coated with glazed sugar.

Miles found himself riding drag all by himself while Tad rode up and down both flanks and helped turn the herd toward Oklahoma. Miles kept the cattle in the lead close-packed and had no trouble. Still, he was relieved when Tad finally joined him in midafternoon. They had not stopped for lunch, but chewed on hardtack and beef jerky, washed down with water from their wooden canteens.

"I been lookin' at that sky," Tad said when he rode up. "Up north and west."

"Yeah. Looks blue and peaceful to me."

"Way off yonder, I think I seen some black wisps. There could be a storm building."

Miles looked again and saw just the faintest dark cloud so far off he thought his eyes might be playing tricks on him.

"See it?" Tad asked.

"Looks like a far-off hill to me."

"It's a cloud. Anyway, we got to get these cattle up to the Canadian for a drink, and I'll be able to tell more when we get there."

"Like what, Tad?"

"How fast the river's runnin', how much water's in it, and where we can cross 'thout drownin' half the herd."

"If you say so," Miles said.

They made twenty miles that day and the cattle were groaning from hunger and thirst, some of them bellowing and the others beginning to toss their horns and trying to break out.

Tad turned the herd northward and they reached the Canadian before sunset. The cattle lined up along the bank and slaked their thirst. Tad rode up and down a stretch of riverbank and came back in a half hour. The hands were all riding back and forth, keeping eyes on the herd. Some of the cattle had finished drinking and were grazing on the grass, seemingly contented.

"There's a small bend about a half mile downriver," Tad told Miles. "Water's not to my liking. It's pretty swift, but I think we can ford it okay. I'll let Newgate run the chuck wagon across first and see how he does."

"If you think that'll work," Miles said.

"If it don't, we're up shit crick 'thout a paddle," Tad said.

Tad rode over close to the drinking cattle. He cupped his hands together and yelled his orders to the cowhands.

"Boys, we'll cross this river and eat supper on the other side. You be ready to drive the herd downstream when I tell you to, in small bunches, a few at a time. Got that?"

The men yelled and nodded.

"Carey, follow me in that chuck wagon," Tad said, and rode off toward the place he had picked as a ford.

Carey clucked to the two horses pulling the wagon, and with a clanking and a rumbling of wheels, the wagon lurched into motion. Miles followed to see how well the wagon made the crossing.

"You go straight across here," Tad told Newgate. "Don't stop. Don't let the horses take the bits in their mouths. You got to keep 'em straight and steady. Can you do it?"

"I sure hope so," Newgate said. He

snapped the reins across the horses' backs, and despite their reluctance, they stepped off the bank into the swift-running waters of the river. The water came up to the hub nuts of the wagon, then rumbled across a thin sandbar and back into deeper water. The horses tried to turn away, but Carey kept them on a straight course, using the buggy whip whenever they tended to go right or left. Their eyes rolled in their sockets and they whinnied their displeasure. But they mounted the far bank and pulled the dripping wagon up on solid ground.

"He did it," Miles exclaimed.

"If he did it, them cows can do it," Tad said. Then he called across the river to Newgate.

"Drive that wagon a good half mile away from the river. Find us a good spot to bed the herd down and where you can fix us some grub for supper. Hear?"

"I hear ya," Newgate replied, and started the wagon rolling again, away from the river.

Miles and Tad rode back to where the men and cattle were waiting.

"Miles," Tad said, "you get behind where I mark the first bunch and ride drag once we get 'em started toward that bend. Then, when they've all crossed all right, you come back and do the same with the next bunch."

Miles nodded that he understood.

Tad walked along and sliced his hand in the air to show where each bunch ended and the next started.

"Pedro," he said, "you get that first bunch I marked off started. I'll help you."

There were about two hundred head in each bunch. Pedro got his bunch started downriver. Miles fell in behind, while Tad rode flank. At the ford, Tad and Pedro cut into the herd, forcing the leaders into the river, then pushed at the others with their horses. Once they started, the cattle made a beeline for the opposite shore, with only one or two drifting into deeper water where they had to swim. Still, they all made it.

"Find a place to bed 'em down, Pedro," Tad called. "There's more a-comin'."

The next bunch was more difficult and Tad had to ride one flank while Curly Bob pushed the leaders to cross in a straight line.

Tad did the same with each bunch, with men riding back across to help run the two hundred head in each bunch across the river. The last bunch followed fast on the heels of the preceding bunch and made the crossing without incident.

Finally, Miles and Tad rode across. On the other side, Tad stopped and pointed to the river.

"Look at it," he said. "See anything different about it?"

Miles looked upriver and at the opposite bank.

"It seems to be rising slightly," he said.

"And look at what's swirlin' out there. Branches and leaves and clumps of stuff. Now that sky is plumb full of black clouds way off. That storm's already hit upriver and it's a-comin' our way with a real gully washer afore mornin'."

Miles looked at the western sky. The sun was still shining and falling slowly toward the distant horizon, but huge black clouds were encroaching on the light, blotting out the blue in one corner of the sky. They seemed to drift from the northwest, growing larger and moving toward them ever so slowly.

"What will we do?" Miles asked.

"Well, we can't run and we can't hide, Miles," Tad said. "All we can do is sing to that herd. If it starts thunderin' and lightnin', they might stampede and we got to do roundup all over again."

"Jesus," Miles said.

"Yeah, a little prayin' might help," Tad said as he turned his horse to follow the herd.

A while later, they all felt the wind rise and blow cold across the prairie. The sky turned black along the eastern horizon, and the glow of the sun faded after it sank from sight. The men all put on their heavy jackets and broke out their slickers before they filled their plates with grub from the chuck wagon.

The cattle moaned and lifted their noses to sniff the air.

The air began to turn slightly moist with the hint of rain as the cattle fed on the tall grasses, their rumps turned westward into the building wind.

CHAPTER 13

Paco Villareal gave crisp, clear orders to his men. He knew they would grumble, but they would get the job done.

"You see that sky?" he said to Bernie James, Al Corning, and Chet Loomis.

"Yeah, we see it," Chet said with a dry Texas twang to his voice. "Means we got a storm comin' in the morning."

"That is what we in Sonora, we Mexicans, call a *feo* sky. *Un cielo muy feo.*"

"You gonna start talkin' Mex, Paco," Al said, "I'm lightin' out for Canada."

The men all laughed, including Roy Leeds, who listened with interest now that his small herd was bedded down and two other riders were already making the rounds on night herd.

"That means that is an ugly sky, *caballeros,*" Paco said, a visible shadow playing on his lips.

"He's a-callin' us *caballeros,*" Bernie

119

cracked. "I think that's somebody who shovels horse shit."

The men around Paco all laughed again, including Roy, but Paco kept his face impassive, except for that trace of mirth puckering his lips.

"Laugh now," Paco said, "because I am going to ask all of you to start rounding up a thousand head of Lazy J cattle and bed them down with this little herd right here."

"At night, with them black clouds blowin' right down on top of us?" Al said as he looked up at the western sky.

"Orders from the big boss, Jared. He wants a herd ready to move down to the Canadian and head east by sunup," Paco said.

"Shit," Chet said. The others uttered similar epithets.

"You will have plenty of light to see," Paco said, "because you will be putting trail brands on those cattle before you bring them down here."

"Impossible," Al said.

The other men grumbled and shook their heads.

"I will do the branding," Paco said. "Murphy, our smithy, is making the irons right now. Roy here will help me."

He turned to Roy, who, though startled,

nodded. "I'll help you, Paco," he said.

"We got to organize this night gather," Paco said. "Brand two heads at a time and run them down here in one long line until we have a thousand head ready to run up to Salina, Kansas. Now. We go."

With that, Paco led the procession up to the quadrant where more than a thousand head of cattle grazed or bedded down. Roy rode alongside him.

"You're asking a lot of your men, Paco, you don't mind me sayin' so."

"We will work all night, Roy, that is true. But I do not think we will drive a herd in the morning. We will be lucky if we can start on the trail by the afternoon."

"You mean the storm?"

"Yes. The storm will be very bad. I have seen such storms before. Those black clouds are not only full with rain, but they will carry loud thunder and the big lightnings. I think it will be very hard to gather and brand that many cows by morning and drive them to this place."

"So why not wait a day? Wait until the storm has passed?"

"Because Jared he say that we must get the herd to Salina before the first day of June. And we already see the month of April slip into May very soon."

"Where did you learn to speak English so good, Paco?" Roy asked.

"Ah, you think I speak the English good, eh? My mother was a schoolteacher, first in Sonora, and then we moved to San Antonio. But I have two tongues and sometimes I think one is better to speak than the other."

"Your mother was American?"

"She was half American, half Spanish. She was not *Mexicana*. She spoke the Castilian tongue, but she could speak the good Mexican as well."

"You are very fortunate, Paco," Roy said.

"Now you must tell me why everyone calls Mr. Blaine, the father of Jared, 'Doc.' Is he *un medico* — I mean to say, a doctor?"

Roy laughed. "Not really. His name is really Delmer, but people started calling him 'Doc' during the war. In fact, at the end of the war."

"The War Between the States? The Civil War?"

"Some call it a civil war. It wasn't civil. Most Texans call it the War Between the States."

"Yes, I know. So, how did Mr. Blaine come to be called 'Doc'?"

"There was a big battle down on the Gulf. Some hill, they say. There was fighting on both sides of the border. Doc was caught in the cross fire. His captain was hit in the leg by artillery fire. They were pinned down for some days, I heard.

"Anyway, Doc carried this big bowie knife and the lieutenant's foot started to rot with gangrene. Doc cut off his foot and packed it with mud and stuff, and when the surgeons saw what he had done, they said he should have been a doctor. And so the men he fought with started calling him 'Doc.' The name stuck and so that's what we call him."

"That is a good story," Paco said.

"And a true one."

They saw a fire in the distance, and when the two men rode up, they saw men standing around it. There were two branding irons buried in the fire's coals, and a man wearing a leather apron and hobnailed boots, with a large mustache, carrot-colored hair, and twinkling blue eyes staring up at them.

"Roy, this is Sean Murphy," Paco said as they dismounted. "He is our blacksmith. He shoes the horses, makes the branding irons, and fixes the wagons."

"Roy, is it? You must be Doc's *segundo*, from what these Irish ears are hearin'." Sean spoke in a soft brogue that came from county Cork, and sported an impish grin that might have been inherited from a leprechaun. He was a short man with large hands and bulging arms that belied a somewhat sunken chest bristling with copper wires.

"A pleasure, Sean."

"Ah, call me Paddy, Roy. To these Texicans, all Irishmen are Paddies. Dunno why."

Roy laughed.

The other men rode up and Paco sent them out into the herd. Roy noticed that there was a chuck wagon parked nearby and a fire going there as well.

"You ready, Paddy?" Paco asked.

"Ready for what?"

"For me and Roy to start putting trail brands on the cattle."

"Oh, sure, Paco, sure," Paddy said. "See?" He pulled one of the irons from the fire and held it so close to Paco's face he had to back away and hold up his hands in mock fearfulness.

"A P?" Paco said.

"Sure, a P for Perryton, and maybe a P for Paco. Jared wanted one letter of the blitherin' alphabet and I could curl a P better'n I ever did the Lazy J."

"You are full of the bullshit, Paddy," Paco said with a laugh.

Paddy shoved the iron back in the fire.

In a few moments, Roy heard the sound

124

of approaching hoofbeats. Beyond the firelight he saw the bobbing heads of white-faced cattle coming their way braced by two flankers. He walked to the fire and slipped on heavy gloves he drew from his back pocket. He grabbed an iron and stood ready.

Paco grabbed the other iron with his bare hands.

"We will brand them as they come by. Paddy will hold them long enough to brand."

To Roy's surprise, Paddy walked a few feet away and picked something up off the ground. It looked like a bracket made of iron. It was just wide enough to fit over a cow's chest or boss. He stood with it between his legs, both hands gripping the long bars that jutted from one side of the bracket.

"Ever done this before, Paddy?" Roy asked.

"I tried it out this afternoon. Got knocked down a few times, but learnt how to brace meself and push. Like so."

He stopped the first cow and bent over, pushing as Paco slammed the iron onto the cow's hip. Paddy pulled away and readied himself for the next one.

"Well, I'll be damned," Roy said, and stepped up to brand a cow that ran into Paddy's makeshift bracket.

125

It was long, slow, torturous work and some of the brands were cockeyed and half burned into hide and hair. But the cattle kept coming and the rain clouds came closer.

Far off, they could see the silent lightning stitching silvery latticework inside the bulging billows of dark thunderheads, and there, far off, was the faint muttering of thunder.

Men kept the fire blazing and grabbed ham sandwiches off the chuck wagon and rode back into the darkness to round up more cattle as the clouds began to blot out the Milky Way and smother the moon until the sky turned pitch-black and the murmurs of thunder turned to loud rumbles that rolled across the sky like falling tenpins in an empty attic.

CHAPTER 14

Not long after Roy and Paco began branding, the two men halted. Several men on horseback appeared out of the darkness. They dragged two old high-sided wagon beds and placed them end to end near the branding fire.

"Here's that chute you asked for, Paco," one of the men said when the beds were in place. "Should make it easier on old Paddy there, who looks plumb tuckered."

"You took your sweet time, Becker," Paco said, a grin on his face.

"Had to take the axles off when we come upon that sump back yonder," Becker said.

"You, Morris, Jesse, and Corny can lend a hand. Go find Al and tell him to start the branded cattle down to the range where the Slash B cattle are bunched. Then come back for more."

"Sure, boss," Will Becker said. "Glad we could oblige."

Paco shooed him and the other riders away with a playful wave of his hand. Then he called out to Chet and the others, "We got us a chute, boys. Run 'em down here in bunches of ten."

The branding went a lot more smoothly with the chutes in place. Roy watched as Paddy worked a hinged board that stopped the cattle inside the wagon beds, which he could drop when they were all branded.

A little after midnight, Jared showed up, riding a sleek black trotter with a blaze face and three white stockings. He had his bedroll wrapped in a yellow slicker behind the cantle of his saddle and was wearing work clothes and riding gloves of soft black kid, a black Stetson with a flat crown, two pistols, and a Winchester jutting from his saddle scabbard.

"Howdy, boys," Jared said as he swung down out of the saddle and ground-tied his horse. "Need an extry hand?"

"You can spell Roy there, Jared, if you like," Paco said.

Roy's face was orange in the firelight and his forehead gleamed with sweat. He grinned.

"What makes you think I need to be spelled?" he said to Paco.

"You branded Paddy in that last bunch,"

joked Paco. "Square on his Irish rump."

Roy stepped away from the chute and planted his iron in the coals. Jared picked it up after a few seconds and held it up to the firelight.

"That's a mighty small P, Paddy," he said.

"It's just a trail brand, Jared," Paddy said. "We don't need to kill the cows with a bigger one."

"What's the 'P' for?" Jared asked.

"Perryton," Paddy said.

"Are you sure?" Jared said. "Folks might mistake that 'P' for Paddy, you reckon?"

"If you keep raggin' on me, Jared Blaine," Paddy said, "it's a-goin' to stand for 'piss on you.' "

Jared laughed louder than Paco and Roy, but he put the hot iron to two head of cattle in the chute and finished off the bunch.

"You keepin' a tally, Paco?" Jared asked.

"I figger we got more than three hundred head wearing trail brands. We'll get a better tally in the morning."

"Slow going," Jared said.

"It will go faster now that we have the wagon beds," Paco said. He plunked the brand back in the fire and wiped the sweat from his face with a bandanna he kept in his back pocket.

Pedro and Bernie ran another dozen head

into the chute and held them in.

"Take a break, boys," Jared said. "We got enough hands now to finish before that storm hits us."

"Thanks, boss," Bernie said. "The rest of the herd's getting mighty restless what with the lightnin' and the thunder."

Jared looked off at the sky. The thunder had grown louder and lightning streaked through the bowels of the black clouds. There was a smell in the air, a smell like the ocean at Galveston, and the wind was starting to pick up. Pieces of broken grass and little wisps of sand blew past them. The flames in the branding fire whipped and lashed with the stronger gusts.

Paco and Jared finished branding the cattle in the chute. Paco held up his hand when Chet showed up with a half dozen steers. The cattle looked wild-eyed and spooked, tossing their heads and trying to turn and rejoin the herd. Chet checked their every move.

"Take a break," Jared told him.

"You want me to run these into them wagon boxes?"

"Run 'em in, but if they get out, we'll let 'em go."

"I could use some hot coffee," Chet said, eyeing the chuck wagon, its canvas top fluttering in the wind, a whitish glare in the dancing firelight.

"We'll join you," Jared said. "I'm buyin'."

They gathered around the chuck wagon, drank from the tin cups Cookie had handed them. The smell of Arbuckles' coffee was strong in the air, mingling with the heady scent of cow shit and steaming horse apples.

Roy sat down on the ground, his back to a wagon wheel. He blew on his coffee, took a sip. He detected the faint taste of cinnamon and it was pleasurable. Arbuckles put a stick of cinnamon in every can and sack of their ground coffee.

Jared sat down near him, stretching out his legs and scraping the ground with the blunt rowels of his spurs until he was comfortable.

"You have a lot of hands, Jared," Roy said. "More'n we got at the Slash B."

"Well, Pa don't have as much land as me and not near as many cattle. He ain't been doin' so good the last coupla years."

"No, he hasn't," Roy said. "But he thinks this drive will help him pay off his mortgage and hopes he'll take a bigger herd to Salina or Abilene maybe next year."

"I hope it happens," Jared said wistfully. "But Pa won't accept no help from me."

Roy didn't say anything. He knew that

131

Doc favored Miles over Jared and figured it had something to do with Miles's wife and Jared's notorious temper.

He looked at the six-guns on Jared's hips. They were .45 Colt revolvers and the grips looked to be mother-of-pearl, not ivory. Still, they were handsome pistols and the grips stood out against the black of Jared's dyed denim work shirt.

"You're packin' a lot of iron, Jared," Roy commented as he brought the tin cup up to his lips again. "Expectin' trouble on the drive?"

"You met Will Becker?"

"Yeah. Briefly."

"Becker just got back from Leavenworth. He's got a sister there and she took sick. He said he had to dodge rustlers and renegade Kiowas all across Kansas. He talked to some of the ranchers and they were hoppin' mad at the lawlessness. He said all the trails were dangerous, with bandits, Injuns, and highwaymen all lookin' for easy prey."

"I wonder if Doc knows about this," Roy said.

"He knows some of it. But Will Becker just got back yesterday and his hair was still standin' on end when he rode up."

"We'll have to keep our eyes peeled," Roy said. "You know which trail you'll take yet?"

"Yeah, I been over the maps. We'll foller the Canadian with plenty of grass and water, then mosey up out of Oklahoma into Kansas, skirt Dodge, and head straight northeast to Salina."

"Lots of rivers to cross," Roy said.

"Can't be helped none, Roy. Cattle got to drink and chew grass."

"You figure you can make it to Salina before the first of June?"

"Well, we can't run the cattle to death, but we ought to beat that deadline by a few days by my reckon'. It all depends on . . ."

Jared didn't finish his sentence. Instead, he sipped from his coffee cup and stared off at the western sky.

A gust of wind blew a tumbleweed past the chuck wagon and it rolled to the make-shift corral and stuck there like some ghostly skeleton. Somewhere, off to the west, a coyote yipped and the fireflies disappeared into the night sky.

Thunder boomed, and pealed in a rolling rumble. Light streaked through the clouds in a dazzling silver display that raked the earth.

"Might be hail in that storm," Jared said. "That'll play hob with us tryin' to bed down the herd."

"I've seen rabbits and quail knocked cold

133

by hail no bigger'n a dime," Roy said.

"And I've seen calves coldcocked by hail the size of baseballs, knocked plumb dead where they stood."

"I guess this will be our first big spring storm," Roy said.

Jared finished his coffee and stood up. "We better get to it. I give that storm another four or five hours before it hits us. It's slow movin' and we'll likely have to swim out of it before it's over."

Roy stood up and tossed the teaspoon of coffee still left in his cup onto the ground. He handed the empty cup to Cookie.

"Let's get to it, boys," Jared said. "Get your thumbs out of your butts."

They all walked back to the branding fire. Paddy picked up the tumbleweed and flung it into the fire. It crackled and sparked and disintegrated into ash before it disappeared.

The men all worked with precision and the branding continued while the wind began to roar and threaten to blow out the fire. Men came and went as they drove cattle down to what had become the main herd and returned for more.

"You got a tally, Paco?" Jared asked as the first patters of rain began to spatter them.

"I figure we've branded better than a thousand head by now, Jared."

"That's what I figger. Paddy, you put out the fire, tell Cookie to roll that wagon down to where we got the herd bedded down."

"May the wind always blow at your back, Jared, darlin'," Paddy said, and began to pull the irons from the fire.

Jared, along with Paco and Roy, drove the last twenty head as the other men rode on to look after the herd.

By the time they reached the bedding grounds, the rain was slashing at them in lancing sheets. Hats blew off and disappeared, slickers flapped like wet sails on a schooner, and the cattle moaned and bawled as riders kept them bunched and turned their backs to the wind.

Puddles began to form on the ground, and rivulets of water ran into the herd, shining bright with every flash of lightning. Thunder deafened their ears, and bunches of cattle rose to their feet and had to be restrained from bolting for high ground that did not exist. No one spoke, but rode their horses hunkered over their saddle horns like monks in yellow robes begging for alms in a merciless universe that was black as pitchblende and electric with jagged streaks of lightning that could kill man, horse, or cow with a direct hit.

Jared raised his wet face to the sky and

shook his fist.

"Damn you," he yelled at the top of his voice, but the wind snatched his words away as if they were birds swept off a tropical limb in a typhoon.

CHAPTER 15

Joadie Lee Bostwick had an uncomfortable feeling in the pit of his stomach. A man had died in that place. His blood still stained the earth, but the man was gone. One of the Gallegos brothers, he didn't know which one. Doc had shot him and now the tracks around the spot where the man had died told some of the story.

Doc and Curly Bob Naylor sat their horses several yards away. Curly had rolled a cigarette and was smoking it. Doc chewed on an unlit cheroot, his eyes full of an almost incomprehensible sadness, that same look Joadie Lee had seen on his face after they had hanged the horse thief. Now he felt some of that sadness in himself. He rode over to where Doc and Curly Bob waited.

"His brothers come and took him away, looks like," he said to Doc, his voice soft and whispery, rough with the gravel of the sadness he felt.

"So they came back," Curly Bob said.

"Looks like," Joadie Lee said. He pulled the makings out of his shirt pocket and flipped open the small container of papers. He began to roll a cigarette and noticed that his hands trembled. In some ways it was easier to take when he saw the body of the man Doc had shot. There was a reality to that which he could understand. The man had tried to kill Doc and Doc had shot him. Joadie Lee had seen dead men before, in the war, and since, when his cousin drowned in the Nueces when they were both young boys.

"It gave me a funny feelin'," Joadie Lee said, "seein' where that boy died."

"I know what you mean," Doc said. "I used to get that feelin' when I was in the war. Seein' where a man had died, sometimes good friends, it, well, it kind of changes the land. The wildflowers lose their colors and the dirt gets real drab as if someone had sprinkled poison on an ant colony. Something goes out of the land in those spots, something you can never get back."

Both Joadie Lee and Curly Bob seemed surprised at what Doc had said and they both went silent.

"Let's get on home," Doc said. They all

heard the rumbling thunder in the distance, and when the dark clouds moved in and blocked out the sun, they rode in near darkness, with the light playing tricks on their eyes. Jackrabbits jumped up and raced off, startling the horses, and lizards slid off rocks that suddenly turned shady. Lightning crackled in the clouds with a sizzling of silver streaks that set off more thunder and lit the land like a photographer's flash powder.

"I never should have hanged that Gallegos boy," Doc said after a while. "I should have just given him a good larrupin' and sent him on home."

"You didn't do nothin' wrong, Doc," Curly Bob said. "That boy stole your horses. That's a hangin' offense most anywheres."

"I could have shown some mercy," Doc said. "Might have been best to let the boy live."

Neither Curly Bob nor Joadie Lee made any comment, as if each man had his own thoughts about horse stealing, justice, and what that hanging had brought down on all of them.

The wind surged up out of the northwest and blew down on them. A few minutes later, the first smattering of rain pocked the dirt and stung their faces. They broke out their yellow slickers and donned them just before the drenching rain struck. The drops clattered off their raincoats and stung their horses' eyes and their own. The wind blew sheets of heavy rain at them until the trail and all the hoof prints were washed away as if none had ever passed that way.

It was near nightfall when Doc rode up to the house with its windows glowing with yellow lamplight. He waved to the boys in the rain as they rode off toward the bunkhouse and stables. He put Sandy up in a three-horse shelter next to the house, stripped him of saddle, bridle, saddlebags, and bedroll, grained him, and forked hay into one of the slatted bins. He poured water into the trough and spoke to the two other horses, which whickered at him and Sandy. He put his gear inside the small tack room in the stable and shut the door, slipping a wooden peg in the latch. He walked to the house and entered by the back door. He hung up his slicker and slapped the water off his hat brim before he went into the kitchen, where the smell of food made his stomach jump.

"I knowed it was you, Doc, when you rode up. I seen your shadder and the boys, and just knowed you had come back."

"Smells good in here," he said.

"You hungry?"

"I could eat the south end of a north-bound polecat right about now," he said.

Ethyl laughed, as she always did at her husband's jokes.

"Well, you just set yourself at the table and I'll get the vittles. You can wash in that basin there on the sink, and I laid out a towel for you."

"Ethyl, what in hell would I do without you?"

"You'd have to shine your own boots — that's what," she said, her voice jovial, a smile of satisfaction flickering on her lips. The sound of the rain on the roof made the kitchen seem cozy and warm and neither of them minded the husky howl of the wind against the clapboard exterior of the frame house. The wind keened in the eaves and whistled as it sniffed at their windows like some prowling beast.

"I do shine my own boots," he said as he laved his hands in the bowl of soapy water. He rinsed them off and dried them with the towel Ethyl had set out.

"Not always," she said.

"Yeah, on Sunday-go-to-meetin's or funerals."

"I'm glad you're back home, Doc. You made good time. I didn't expect you until maybe late tonight or early in the mornin'. Jared doin' all right?"

"He was fine. He'll make the drive. I left Roy with him. We lost a few head."

"Anything else happen?" she asked, and there was something mysterious about her question that made the hackles rise on the back of his neck. But he knew she couldn't know what had happened on the drive up to Jared's. Nobody knew, except he and his men.

"Nope," he lied.

He didn't want to tell her about the run-in with the Gallegos boys and, especially, he didn't want her to know that he had shot and killed one of them. Oh, he would tell her sometime, but not now, not when he was hungry as a bear coming out of hibernation and just getting back home and all.

"You sure?" she said as she took plates from the cupboard, then opened a drawer and splashed silverware atop them with a tinny clatter.

"Real sure, darlin'."

She looked at him. And he knew she knew that he was holding something back. She wasn't a mind reader, but she knew him, knew his ways. She could, in fact, read him like a book.

But she said nothing. She just smiled at

him with that knowing smirk of hers and tossed her head as if to shake off his lie.

He saw her carrying plates into the next room, and his eyebrows arched. They hardly ever ate supper in the dining room. They mostly ate there when they had company.

"Where you goin'?" he asked. He walked over to the kitchen table in the center of the room. "Kitchen's fine with me."

"We got company," she said, and vanished through the doorway.

"Company?"

"You come on in, Doc, and try not to say anything until you hear all I know."

Doc followed her into the dining room and was surprised to see Caroline sitting at the table. She was slumped over and he could not see her face. But there were bandages on her arms and another wrapped around her head like a turban. There was blood on the bandages.

"Christ," he said. "What happened to Caroline?"

"Now, Doc, you just sit down while I get our vittles and I'll tell you all about it. I'm going to set the coffee on to boil now that you're here and if you need some brandy after you've et, I set a bottle out in the front room."

Doc sat down in a daze.

"Caroline?" he said as Ethyl set out three plates and put the silverware beside each pewter plate. She left without speaking to carry in the supper she had prepared.

Caroline moaned and tried to raise her head.

"My God," he said, "what happened to you, girl?"

Ethyl came with platters of roast beef, boiled potatoes, red beans, and collard greens. She set the food on the table.

"I didn't make no gravy, but they's butter if you want it for your taters," she said as she sat down. "You can pour your water out of that pitcher there. Coffee's on the stove."

Doc shook his head.

"What happened to Caroline?" he said.

"Fill your plate, Doc," Ethyl ordered, as if Caroline were not there. She put a small cut of beef and half a boiled potato on Caroline's plate and filled her water glass.

"Ethyl, damn it, are you going to tell me what's wrong with Caroline? She looks like she's been in a fight."

Ethyl ignored him. She reached over and tilted Caroline's head up. Doc reared back in shock. Her face was covered with welts and bruises. Both her eyes were blackened as if she had been mauled by a prizefighter. One cheekbone was swollen and red with the blue outlines of veins streaming into her jowls. Her lips were puffed and split, the cracks a bright crimson.

Caroline opened her mouth and winced from the pain. Ethyl spooned a small piece of meat into her mouth.

"Now, you try and chew that meat, Caroline," Ethyl said in a voice that she might have used on a baby or a small child. "You need to build up your strength."

Caroline made a sound. It was a guttural noise that sounded to Doc like something coming from an animal's throat. It was half moan and half groan and it tore at him, rattled his senses since he could feel the pain in her voice. Hell, he could see the pain on her face. Pain painted her face into a hideous mask that was all crooked and warped and twisted into some grotesque caricature of a living person.

Caroline did not chew the piece of meat, but it fell back in her throat and she began to choke. Ethyl rose from her chair and slapped Caroline on her back. Caroline gagged, but drew in a breath and the blue pallor fled from her face as the meat went down into her stomach.

"My God, Ethyl, she can't eat. She'll choke to death if you try to feed her."

"I gave her broth a while ago. She ain't

145

been here long, about a hour or two, I reckon. Poor thing."

"I can't eat a bite of this damned food until you tell me what happened to our daughter." He almost choked on the last word, because he had long since stopped calling her kin because of the rift Caroline had caused between their two sons.

"You'd better eat, Doc, because you're not going to like any of it. This poor girl's been knocked senseless and I mean senseless. I tried to talk to her, but she just babbles like some idiot in a madhouse."

"You think she — she's mad?" he gasped.

"As a hatter, Doc."

Caroline's head sagged and lolled against her shoulder. She looked up at him with a crooked smile. But her eyes were empty. There was nothing in them but smoke and vacancy, as if her soul had been sucked out of her and all that was left, sitting like a scarecrow in that chair, was a shell, an empty shell of a person.

Caroline was still breathing, but she looked to Doc as dead as those soldiers down on the Gulf, dead men with empty eyes, staring into nothingness, into an eternity that he could never understand.

CHAPTER 16

Jared braced himself when the first strong gust of rain-borne wind drenched him. He struggled to stay on his feet and reached out to grab Roy's shoulder to keep from falling. Roy was leaning into the wind and had trouble keeping his footing. The driving rain stung both men's eyes and blinded them until they bowed their heads and turned away from the onslaught.

Jared drew Roy close so that he could shout into his ear and be heard above the roar of thunder and wind, the thick curtains of rain that swept over them.

"A hell of a way to start a drive, Roy," Jared yelled.

Roy turned his head to answer Jared. "This is west Texas. What did you expect?"

"In Kansas this could be a twister," Jared shouted back, and the two men staggered toward the chuck wagon to escape the brunt of the wind. Cookie, with the help of some other hands, had driven stakes in the ground and tied ropes to the wagon. The horses were also roped tight to iron stakes so that they wouldn't run off to escape the storm.

Lightning flashed and thunder pealed in mighty rumbles across the black sky. Other men appeared out of the darkness and crammed themselves against Roy and Jared. There was Becker, Morris, and James.

"Where in hell is Paco?" Jared asked Becker.

"Him and Al are movin' some of the cattle to higher ground," Becker said. "I mean it's runnin' rivers out there."

"There ain't much high ground," Jared said.

"You know where them live oaks is all clumped up on a hill? That's the high ground in this mess."

A hand lifted the side flap on the chuck wagon. Cookie, whose actual name was Vincent Oliphant, peered out.

"I thought this was high ground," Cookie said.

"On wheels, it is," Jared said. "You'd better just hope this wagon floats."

"I made sandwiches, if anybody wants them," Oliphant said.

"They'll get soggy," Becker said.

The flap closed and they all heard, dimly,

the clank of pots and pans as Cookie settled himself onto his bedding.

"If this is as bad as it gets, we'll be all right by morning," Roy said.

No sooner were his words out of his mouth than they heard bellows from the cattle. The horses whinnied in high-pitched ribbons of bloodcurdling screams. The canvas on the wagon shook with drumlike tattoos. The men all bent down under the onslaught of hail the size of mothballs. They hunkered down and duck-waddled under the wagon to escape the pelting of hailstones.

The hail did not last long, but the ground was covered with white balls. The wind howled for another hour or two and began to abate before morning. When the men walked out to mount their horses, the rain came down in torrents. The ground was littered with dead crows and prairie chickens, jackrabbits, drowned rattlesnakes, and field mice. The groggy cows stood in disconsolate bunches, silent as lambs as the riders rode among them.

Paco and Al rode out from the grove of oaks to greet them, shadowy drenched figures on horseback, their yellow slickers barely visible through the rain and darkness.

"No flash floods that I could see, Jared," Paco said. "Hail tore a lot of leaves off them trees."

"We lose any cattle that you know of?" Jared asked.

"None run off, far as I know."

Jared and Roy made a quick head count as they circled the bunched cattle, streaming in and out of their ranks and humming off-key tunes to reassure the animals.

"I reckon we got better'n two hundred and fifty-five head," Jared said.

"I make it two sixty," Roy said.

"Close enough."

The rain swept past them in the early hours before dawn and there was a creamy fissure in the eastern sky when they got the herd moving. Cattle and horses sloshed through mud and puddles, skirting small rivers that coursed through gullies and arroyos and gushed out of them in murky, muddy gushers that petered out as the water spread and sank into drier ground.

The Canadian was over its banks, roaring past them as they traversed its northern bank. The waters were full of dead animals, tree branches shorn of leaves, deadwood, and clumps of dirt torn from the banks that bobbed and sank until they were decimated into shards of grass and disintegrating dirt.

The sun was a feeble glow as it rose to a precarious position behind streamers of dark clouds and finally disappeared as the black clouds of night rolled on into the day far to the east.

The chuck wagon rumbled along behind the herd, its wheels occasionally sinking into mud, then jerking loose as Cookie rattled the reins and cracked the buggy whip. Riders came and went, taking sandwiches from a side cabinet that Cookie had filled before setting out. The rain let up and a drizzle set in that was dissipated by noon. The cattle trudged on, following Paco's lead, eyeing the river with baleful eyes, sometimes stopping to drink from a stand of leftover rainwater.

Late in the afternoon, Paco saw something not far from the banks of the Canadian that disturbed him. He called to Al, who was riding flank some hundred or so yards behind the head of the herd.

"Al, go see what that is over there. Looks like one of our cows."

"Can't be," Al said. "Less'n some broke loose last night and run on up ahead."

"Check it out," Paco said.

Al rode down to the river and disappeared from sight. The herd kept moving now that the land was drying up, and grass, beaten down by the hail, had sprung back to life. Cows grabbed clumps of grass as they passed, barely pausing to jerk the shoots loose, and chewed on the fodder while they continued to move forward.

Paco noticed something else while Al was gone. The ground was chewed up, moiled into a mash of loose earth for yards on either side of the herd behind him. The damage was far worse than the hailstorm or wind could have caused and there was little sign of water washing over the hardpan.

Every now and then he saw what looked like a large hoofprint that was too big to be a deer's. More like an elk's, he thought, but he knew there were no elk in that part of Texas, nor any in Oklahoma or Kansas.

Puzzled, he rode on, and the herd followed obediently, urged on by the flankers.

Al returned in a few minutes and told Paco what he had found.

"You'd better ride back and tell Jared," Paco said. "I'll hold the herd until he rides up."

Al rode off while Paco called out to the flankers and began turning the leaders at the head of the herd. He stopped them. The cattle milled and began to graze while the western sky blazed a fiery orange, setting the distant scraps of clouds afire in a glorious sunset.

"I found two dead cows," Al said. "Thought they was ours at first, strays that might have cut loose during the night."

"And were they?" Jared asked. He saw that the herd was slowing, bunching up.

"No, sirree," Al said. "Them cattle was drowned and washed up by the river. Startin' to stink to high heaven."

"Did you check for brands?" Roy asked.

Al nodded. "I sure did. They was wearing two brands, both of 'em. And not the same neither."

"What do you mean?" Jared asked.

"Well, sir, one of 'em bore a Slash B, and the other had a Rockin' M. Both had trail brands. Looked like a Bar A, near as I could tell."

Jared whistled.

"Rocking M is my brother Miles's brand," he said.

"Come see for yourself," Al said.

"Roy, you tend to the drag," Jared said. "I'll be back."

Roy nodded and walked his horse to the rear of the herd just to keep the herd apprised of his presence.

The dead cattle were bloated and gave off a stench of river water and decomposing flesh. Jared examined them closely and climbed back on his horse. He rode over to where Paco was holding the herd in check.

"Them dead cows are from another herd," he told Paco. "One belongs to my pa, the other to my brother."

"There are signs that a large herd passed here a day or so ago, Jared. Look at the ground."

Jared rode off a hundred yards or so and returned, his neck puffing up like a bull's in heat.

"You were right, Paco," he said. "Some son of a bitch is sure as hell drivin' a big herd, heading the same way we are."

"Not your pa," Paco said.

"I think Miles, more likely. We been double-crossed."

"How's that?" Paco asked.

Jared tilted his Stetson back on his head and scratched at the indentation in his hair made by the sweatband.

A pair of mourning doves whistled by, following the course of the river, their gray bodies twisting in the air. Somewhere a bobwhite quail piped a territorial whistle and buzzards began to circle in the sky near the places where the dead cattle lay bloating with sun-warmed gases. Flies zizzed around the two men and the horses flicked at them with their tails.

"I think my pa double-crossed me," Jared said.

"Huh?"

"Oh, I know it sounds crazy, but I wouldn't put it past him."

"You think Miles is taking his own herd to Salina?" Paco asked.

"Yeah, I sure as hell do. Along with some of our pa's cattle. Might be Pa's way of giving us both a chance to make some cash."

"Well, if that don't beat all," Paco said.

Jared squared his hat. "Keep the herd moving until after sundown. Find a good place to bed 'em down. We'll get an early start in the mornin', Paco."

"I'll find us a good place to spend the night."

"Then we're goin' to run 'em like hell. I aim to beat Miles to Salina."

"He's got a head start on you, Jared."

"It's a long trail, Paco."

Jared rode off to the rear of the herd. The cattle started moving before he reached Roy. The distant sky reddened and the gilt-edged clouds began to fade into ashen loaves and puffs of cottony blossoms. There was a soft southerly breeze coming off the river and teal whistled past, blue wings and greenings, their wings whistling like diminutive flutes until they were specks on the paling blue of the sky.

Some of the cattle began lowing as if seeking a place to drop their weight on rain-softened ground.

Roy waved his hat at a steer breaking from the herd. He rode back to Jared, shaking his head.

"He never said a word to me, Jared," Roy said.

"No, he wouldn't. It was all done in secret."

"Your pa's a deep man. He thinks too much sometimes."

"I'd like to beat Miles to Salina," Jared said, "then see the look on Pa's face when he counts out the money."

"I reckon Doc's got his reasons," Roy said lamely. He knew there was a rivalry between the two brothers, but he didn't know how deep it really went. Very deep, he thought, and that could spell trouble if Jared tried to beat Miles to the railhead in Salina.

Big trouble.

CHAPTER 17

Ethyl had to almost force Doc to finish his supper. She did this by threatening not to tell him what had happened to Caroline. As he finished the last of the food and drank a swallow of tea, he looked over at Caroline, whose head had drooped so low her chin rested between the twin globes of her breasts.

"I ain't gonna wait all night, Ethyl. What happened to Caroline? I got me a bellyache from gulpin' down all that food."

Ethyl calmly cleared away the supper dishes while Doc sat there and stewed with impatience. Finally, Ethyl sat down and took Doc's hand in hers.

"Norm Collins and Skeeter Parsons brought her here in one of Miles's wagons just before it started to rain," Ethyl said. "They carried her into the house and I asked Norm what had happened to her. I thought she might have fallen off her horse."

"What did he say?"

"They said that one of Miles's hands had gone to the house after Miles left with his herd. He and Skeeter saw the man go in and later heard a lot of noise and screaming."

"Who went in the house?" Doc asked, although he thought he already knew.

"It was that young whelp, Earl Rawson."

Doc kept silent, listening to her every word.

"According to Skeeter, this Earl started drinking Miles's whiskey and got into a fight with Caroline over something. He started beating her up. Skeeter and Norm came between Earl and Caroline. Earl started to fight with Norm, who knocked him down. Skeeter saw that Caroline was all bloodied and dazed. When neither he nor Norm could get any sensible answers out of her, they brought her here."

"What happened to Rawson?" Doc asked.

"They don't know. He run off and they never saw him again. They're both out at the bunkhouse waiting to see what you have to say about it. I think they want to know what's going to happen to Caroline."

"Did you talk to her?"

"I tried. Doc, she doesn't even know my name. And she doesn't know she's married

158

to Miles. She's just gone plumb dumb. I don't know what to do."

"We'll have to get her to a doctor. Maybe first thing in the morning."

"There's a good one in Amarillo. Maybe he can tell us what's wrong with Caroline."

Doc rose from his chair and walked around the table to Caroline. He leaned down and lifted her head. He looked into her vacant eyes.

"Caroline, it's me, Doc. I'm your father-in-law. Do you remember me?"

Caroline gurgled and made grotesque sounds in her throat.

"I don't think she can talk at all, Doc," Ethyl said.

The rain continued to blow against the house, shaking all the windows. The wind howled outside.

"I'm going out to talk to Norm and Skeeter," Doc said as he let Caroline's head fall back to where it was. "You need help getting Caroline to bed?"

"No, I can handle it. I laid her out in that spare sleeping room when the boys first brought her in. I thought she might feel better if I gave her something to eat. But you can see how she is."

"Yes. It looks like that Rawson kid beat her up pretty bad."

"It's just horrible," Ethyl said.

Doc put on his slicker and walked out to the bunkhouse. Lamps glowed inside and he could see the yellow and crystal rain striking the frame in broad sheets. The wind blew hard when he opened the door and men cried out as wind and rain swept through the long room.

He saw Skeeter playing cards with Randy Eckoff and Dale Walton. The men looked up when Doc approached.

"Where's Norm?" Doc asked.

Skeeter stood up. His eyes were rheumy and he looked tired. His cuffs were still wet, as were his mud-splattered boots.

"Norm went to tell Miles what happened with his wife," Skeeter said. "I told him to wait until the rain stopped, but he wouldn't hear of it."

"Do you know why Rawson beat Caroline half to death, Skeeter?"

"Some argument, I reckon. When me and Norm got inside the house, he had Caroline down on the floor. He was drunker'n seven hunnert dollars, and was choking the poor woman."

"He say anything?"

"He was callin' Caroline a bitch and said he was a-goin' to kill her."

"What happened then?" Doc asked.

"Norm grabbed the kid and jerked him off'n Caroline. I thought she was already dead and got down on my knees and put my ear up to her mouth. She was breathin', but just barely."

"And what did Norm do?"

"Rawson started to fight him. Norm hit him in the mouth with his fist and Rawson run out of the house. Me and Norm got Caroline to breathin' right again, but when we tried to talk to her, she just looked at us as if she had no brains at all."

Doc drew a breath and shook his head. "Then what?"

"I went and got a wagon, one we used to haul wood in. Me and Norm lined it with blankets and pillars and carried her out there. We thought we ought to bring her here so's you could see what Rawson done to her."

"Did she say anything? I mean the whole time you drove up here, did she tell you what happened?"

"Nope," Skeeter said. "Me'n Norm tried talkin' to her every now and then, but she just lay back there in that wagon and moaned. She didn't even cry, Doc. She just moaned like some hurt animal."

Doc swore under his breath. "We'll use that wagon in the morning to take her into

Amarillo. You going to stick around or go back to Dumas?"

"I reckon I'll stick around so's I can find out how she is. No man ought to beat a woman like that."

"Did you know Caroline was messin' around with Rawson?" Doc asked.

The other men in the bunkhouse had gathered around the table and were listening intently to Doc and Skeeter. Doc could hear them breathing under the patter of rain on the roof, which was steady and hard.

"I knowed they was somethin' goin' on twixt them two. Miss Caroline, she had Earl doin' all kinds of chores for her, fixin' one thing or another, and sometimes he'd stay in the house a long time and I didn't hear no hammer poundin'. It was awful quiet them times."

"I saw him leave out the back door the day I came to get Miles to make the drive to Salina," Doc said.

"Yeah. He was supposed to be helpin' with the gather."

"Did Miles know something was going on between his wife and Rawson?" Doc asked.

"He never said nothin', if he did," Skeeter said. He paused, then continued. "I don't think he knew or he would have fired that kid or killed him."

Doc sighed and clapped Skeeter on the shoulder. He looked at the other men, who were all looking at him.

"Let's keep this in the family for now," he said. "But if any of you run across Earl Rawson . . ."

"If we see him, what?" Dale asked.

They all waited for Doc's answer.

"I ought to tell you to clap him in irons and bring him to me so I could beat him half to death with a pole."

"We could do that," Randy said. "With pleasure."

Doc drew in another deep breath. The men could see that his mind was working.

"Any of you see Rawson," Doc said, "you shoot him on sight."

"We might beat him up first," Skeeter said.

"I wouldn't mind if you did, Skeeter," Doc said. "Good night, boys. One way or another, Rawson's going to pay for what he did to my son's wife."

"Hear, hear," the men chorused as Doc walked outside into the rain.

Doc walked slowly back to the house. He wondered what Miles would say if Norm caught up with him and told him what had happened to Caroline.

He wondered too what Jared would say when he found out that the woman he loved was now little more than a vegetable, with no memory, no power of speech, no love left for anyone.

He had never felt such a sadness as he felt now, a sadness for Caroline, for Miles, and even for Ethyl and Jared.

That sadness, he knew, would rob them all of days or years in their lives. He felt very old when he went back into the house, a house so bleak and cold it seemed empty and useless, just like him.

CHAPTER 18

Clarence Ruggles bent to the plow. His muscles rippled in his suntanned arms. Sweat beaded up in the grimy creases of his forehead like sunstruck jewels despite the shade from the brim of his seedy straw hat. His hands gripped the plow handles and he bore down on them as the mule strained to pull him through a rock that had surfaced suddenly in the furrow.

"Gee, Pete," Clarence said, and tugged on the reins that were draped over his shoulder like elongated leather suspenders.

He heard the screech of the iron against the rock, but the mule swerved from its path, and though the furrow was now crooked, it would surely do.

The other fields that bordered the fallow one were already green with corn, milo, and wheat. This was the last big field to plow and plant. It was the largest, more than a square mile, and had not been plowed for a year. The dirt was hard-packed and the moldboard plow was so dull he knew he would have to sharpen it before he finished the field. The mule was sweating and its hide was streaked with blood drawn by the blowflies. It was hot and there was so much field left to plow, Clarence knew he would have to unhitch the mule and turn the plow over in order to file the blade to a necessary sharpness.

He had files in the thin sleeves of his overalls. He unhitched the plow and tilted it on its side. He removed the files from his pocket and sat down, straddling the plow. He started with a rattail file and bore down on it as he raked the sharp edge of the plow. Metal began to gleam as the dirt and dull metal flaked into dusty filings. When he had exposed the entire blade, he switched to a flat file and began to hone the blade to a fine edge. His even strokes were methodical and he could feel his muscles flex and ripple in his arms. His sleeves became sodden with sweat and his hands grew slippery as if they were bathed in oil. Finally, the plow edge was sharp to the touch, and he slipped the files back in his pocket.

He left the plow as it was and walked up to the road to the barn, every muscle in his body aching, his legs rubbery, his footfalls uncertain. He had graded the road with a two-by-twelve weighted down and pulled by Pete so that it was smooth and wide. It bordered that field and the others that lay beyond.

The sun stood straight up in the sky when he slipped the traces next to a watering trough.

"Pete, you can rest while I eat my dinner. I'll bring you back some oats."

The mule tossed its head and its floppy ears bounced up and down like a harlequin's tassels. Clarence tied the reins to a post next to the trough.

He walked along the edge of the field toward the barn. He could see both his house and the nearby barn, but they were small and just barely poked above the horizon. Clarence owned a large farm that he and his sons had homesteaded before the war. Their houses stood empty beyond his own. Now that they were both dead, he and Floybel, his wife of thirty years, were wondering if they should hire help or sell off some of their land.

He thought of his sons often. They had been very dear to him, both born in Virginia while he fought with Lee, first at Manassas Junction and, later, at Gettysburg. He sired one before he went off to fight for the

South, and the other while he was home on leave. After Gettysburg, with a broken heart, he and Floybel journeyed westward with sons Branford and Stanley. He homesteaded 160 acres in Kansas, bought more adjoining land; then when his sons were young men, they homesteaded more acreage, married, and they all worked the farm.

Two years before, both his sons had been killed in a fight with Texas cattlemen who drove their herd onto Ruggles farmland, trampling crops, fouling the creeks, and tearing up their peaceful existence. Stanley had been shot by a trail boss who hailed from Quitaque, Texas, and came north along the Palo Verde Trail. Branford, in a rage after seeing his brother brutally shot, went after his brother's killer on foot. One of the cowmen broke out a lariat, roped the young man, and then rode off at a gallop. He dragged Branford, who kicked and screamed while trying to slip the rope from around his waist. The rope just got tighter and Branford's screams dwindled to short whimpers and finally ceased. His clothes were ripped and torn and so was his face. The cowhand who had roped and dragged him slipped the rope off, coiled it back up, and attached it to his saddle. The herd moved on, leaving the two Ruggles boys dead. Floybel was inconsolable.

Clarence buried his sons in a plot some distance from the house and planted box elders and maples for shade. He put fresh crosses on their graves every year. He made them out of wood and painted them white, painted their names in black so that they always looked fresh. The boys' wives stayed on for another month and then went back east and sent greetings at Christmas for a year or so, then stopped corresponding altogether.

Both women had remarried and Floybel cried herself to sleep every night for more than a year.

Since then, other cattlemen from Texas had tried to cross their farmland, but Clarence fought them off. He enlisted the help of distant neighbors. These men helped him shoot the lead cattle and turn the herds away. It gave Clarence little satisfaction to shoot and kill cattle, because he still grieved for his sons. But he harbored a deep hatred of cattlemen and Texans. Each time he made the new crosses for his sons' graves, he wept quietly and his rage boiled up in him.

Now he was left with a large farm that was becoming too much for him. His joints ached and he had difficulty getting out of bed in the mornings. Floybel was showing her age too, and much of her former good nature had been wiped away by the deaths of her sons. She still grieved and there were nights when she couldn't sleep and walked the floors of the house, moaning and beating her chest, pulling her long, graying hair. Clarence would find clumps of her hair on the floor in the early morning when he arose to milk the cows with cracked fingers, every joint a painful reminder of his arthritis.

He walked past the hay barn and the smaller milking barn to the well with its trough, set between the house and outbuildings. He worked the pump handle up and down. Water spewed from the spout. He took off his hat and drenched his head, then scrubbed his face and hands. He dried off with a towel hanging on a used hay hook. When he put his hat back on and turned toward the house, he saw Floybel standing on the porch, her apron floating over her plain gray dress with the little white collar that hid the wattles in her neck.

"You be a mite late, Clarence, but the food's still warm and the table's set."

"Are you bein' my clock today, Floybel?" Clarence said.

"You got your old head bent over that plow all mornin', you probably didn't see it," she said. "I been seein' it all mornin' through my kitchen winder."

"What's that?" he asked.

She pointed off to the south.

"That dust cloud yonder," she said. "It keeps getting bigger'n bigger."

He looked at the sky. Way off in the distance, he saw a haze, a thin scrim of reddish dust that hung in the air like rosy smoke.

"Damn," he said.

"Cursin' ain't goin' to help none," she said. "I'm thinkin' one of us ought to take the buggy over to the Bickhams' and see if they can't ride over with some long guns."

He climbed the steps and stood next to her. He put an arm around her waist, but she pulled away.

"We ain't got time for that nonsense, Clarence. You keep your fool hands to yourself."

"Maybe it's just the wind," he said. "I saw some dark clouds to the southeast when I was walkin' back to the barn. Looks like we might get us a storm."

"I seen 'em too," she said. "They ain't no wind here yet and that cloud of red dust is still a far piece. But I'm thinkin' it looks like more of them Texans is comin' and headin' straight for our farm."

"Too far off to tell."

"Well, I think one of us ought to go tell the Bickhams and they can tell the Cramers and the Cramers can get word to the Longleys. We might need a heap of help if more of them Texans is a-comin'."

"You can ride over and tell Jerry Bickham, once we know for sure."

"Might be too late."

Her face was creased with worry lines, her mouth wrinkled like a dried prune, her small green-blue eyes cloudy with worry.

He looked again to the south and saw wisps of dust rise above the tiny reddish cloud. The tendrils did not waft away with wind, but just hung there like strands of rosy cobwebs. He saw the dark clouds to the southwest, just above the distant horizon. There could be a storm coming, he thought, and that sure as hell might be a cattle drive heading their way.

"I got to finish that field before nightfall," he said. "Ground won't wait another day."

"Oh, you and your ground. It waited a year. I think they's trouble comin' up the pike and if you don't turn them Texans away, we're gonna lose what crops we got started."

"Maybe they'll read my signs and turn off," he said.

"Oh, you think Texans can read, huh, Clarence?"

"Now, now, Floybel, don't get yourself into a hissy over a little bit of dust in the sky. If it's a herd of cows, they're more than a day away by my figgerin'. Can't get here much before mornin', I'm thinkin'."

"Well, that may be, but we ought to be ready for them when they gets here, sure enough."

"You take the buggy and ride over to the Bickhams' after dinner," he said. "You should be back long before suppertime."

"I'll do that, Clarence. If you'll hitch up Lady Kay for me."

"The mare? You ought to take the gelding."

"Foxy's too ornery. Lady Kay will carry me where I want to go."

"Suit yourself, Floybel."

They walked into the house together. They left the door open. Clarence could smell the food warming on the stove. The kitchen table was set and she poured him a glass of spring water before she brought the chicken and dumplings she had prepared. There were preserved peaches from their orchards, kept in Mason jars in the storm cellar, and spinach from her garden out back.

"You want milk?" she asked.

"Nope. It sours in my stomach when I'm plowin'," he said.

"Clarence, you work too hard. You got to get a hired man or two to help out."

"Unreliable," he said.

She laughed and sat down, began to dish up the food with a large ladle. Clarence tied his napkin around his neck like a bib and rolled up his sleeves. His bony wrists were tanned and speckled with brown spots.

They bowed their heads when the food was steaming on their plates.

"Lord, we give thanks for this food," Clarence intoned. "And we're grateful for all your blessings. Amen."

"Amen," Floybel said. She raised her head and glanced out the window. She frowned and the worry lines on her forehead deepened as her sea-green eyes danced with a vagrant light that only served to deepen the shadows under them.

The house creaked in the silence as they ate, ticking like some old attic clock covered with dust but refusing to die.

CHAPTER 19

Miles studied the map his father had given him. It was crude, so he had been careful to have one of his hands scout ahead as the herd moved northward. He had also made changes to the map, adding landmark notations and observations of the terrain.

"For future use," he told Roy.

"What you ought to do, Miles," Roy said, "is draw up a new map. Just get a blank piece of paper and draw a line on it. When we're all through with the drive, you can add them notes."

"Just a line?"

"No, you can add cross lines for good or bad places, put dots in for towns or landmarks."

"I ain't no mapmaker," Miles said.

"Neither am I. But if I was makin' a new map, that's how I'd do it."

"I got a map. I'm just adding to it."

"You write so small nobody can read it."

"I can read it," Miles said, and the subject dropped out of their conversation.

They had begun to see distant farmhouses and roads that were not on Doc's map. Miles noted these in his tiny scrawls. So far, they had avoided any encounters with Kansas farmers, but there had been ominous indications that Texas cattlemen were not welcome.

At one place, a crossroads, there was a sign that said NO TEXANS ALLOWED. The cattle had run over it, knocking it to the ground. Randy laughed.

"Did you do that a-purpose?" Dale called out when he saw the sign go down.

"No, Dale," Randy said. "That sign just jumped out in front of the cows on my flank and they tromped it down."

The herd followed a path that paralleled the Arkansas River, plainly marked on the map Miles carried with him, but the drovers had to thin the herd to avoid some of the farmland crops.

"This don't look good, Roy," Miles said. "We're seein' more and more farms and I think the herd just messed up an irrigation canal."

"They run through it," Roy said, "but it was just like crossin' a creek. Water from the river's still runnin'."

"Still, we have to be careful. I don't want to get chased by a lot of farmers with pitchforks and scythes."

"Or get blasted with both barrels of a shotgun," Roy said.

Later that day, Jules and Dale turned the herd to the river. As the cattle lined up to drink, Jules rode to the rear of the column, where he met up with Roy and Miles.

"Miles," Jules said, "you got your glass?"

"In my saddlebag. Why?"

"I see some specks up ahead that might be farm buildings. Can't make 'em out real clear. You want to take a look?"

Miles fished in his saddlebag and brought out an old telescope, studded with brass bindings. He pulled it to its full length and brought it up to his right eye.

"Don't see no smoke," he said.

"Hell, they ain't gonna burn wood in this heat," Jules said.

"I see what looks like maybe a roof. Hold on." He adjusted the eyepiece and swept the lens across a distant point on the horizon. "Might be two roofs. I can make 'em out just barely."

"That's where we got to go," Jules said. "Right straight to them buildings."

Roy reached for the telescope. Miles relinquished it and watched as Roy viewed the objects in the distance.

"Probably a big old farm," Roy said. "We'd better scout it. We won't get there till morning, probably, but we may have to go around it."

"I agree," Miles said.

"I'll send Dale on up ahead to look things over," Jules said.

"Have him report back to me," Miles said.

"Sure thing, boss," Jules said, and rode back to the head of the column.

"You want us to get the herd moving, Miles?" Roy said.

"No, let them drink. They'll move slower and that will give us time to see if that's a farm out yonder. Maybe Dale can find a way around it that won't waste much of our time."

"Good idea," Roy said, and they both watched the cattle as they gulped water from the river.

There was a commotion at the riverbank. Cows bawled and reared up. Some kicked out their hind legs, then ran, bumping into other cattle. A few cows bellowed.

Miles looked over at the site where cattle were rearing up and kicking, and saw several bolt away from the river. Then he heard some splashes and became alarmed.

"Something's got into those cows," Roy

declared, and put the spurs to his horse's flanks. Miles wheeled his horse and followed. Randy yelled and galloped over to the river, flailing his hat in an attempt to drive some of the cattle away from the center of the disturbance.

"You hear that?" Roy said.

Miles listened to a sound that emanated from the bunch of wildly milling cattle.

"Sounds like rain," Miles said. "Rain on leaves."

Randy yelled out as his horse reared up and pawed the air, then hit the ground and went into a tailspin. Randy held on as if he were at a rodeo atop the deck of a bucking bronco.

"Rattlers," Randy shouted. "A whole nest of 'em."

Miles rode up and pushed through the panicked clutch of cows trying to escape the danger. He saw a number of small snakes wriggling toward him, their tails straight up and gyrating in circles. Rattles clattered and snakes struck at the legs and hooves of cattle. The uproar from the bellowing cows nearly drowned out the insistent buzz of the rattles. The snakes were so small, their rattling did sound like rain pelting down on trees, striking the leaves and bark with a steady and monotonous tattoo.

Randy regained control of his horse, and reached for his coiled lariat. The bank had given way under the weight of so many stomping cattle and four had fallen into the river. They were struggling to swim, their front hooves smashing the water like so many millwheels. The cattle were swept along with the current.

Men yelled back and forth as the cattle flailed the water, trying to buck the current and swim back to shore.

Roy grabbed his lariat as Randy whirled his loop into a wider circle above his head. Randy threw the rope and it landed around a cow's neck. His horse backed up and the rope grew taut.

Baby rattlesnakes streamed over the ground like giant diamond-backed worms, their rattles a blur at the end of their tails. The racket increased as Miles unlimbered his own lariat and rode to the bank several yards from where Randy was pulling a heavy whiteface up to the bank, his horse straining with the ponderous weight of the water-logged cow.

Ralph Beasley roped another cow, a large steer, and his horse turned and pulled the rope taut. Ralph rode along the bank and gradually pulled away from it. The steer's hooves struck bottom a foot from shore and it struggled to pull itself up onto dry land. Ralph spurred his horse and the steer gained the bank and clambered up. It dripped water and shook itself. Randy turned and rode up to it, loosened the loop, and freed his rope.

Miles threw down on the last head of a cow that he saw swimming frantically toward the opposite bank. He built his loop and hurled it with all his might. He watched as the lariat sailed past the struggling cow and then dropped over its horns. He jerked on the rope and the cow's head twisted as the lariat tautened, enclosing both horns in its closed loop.

"Come on, Abe," he yelled to his horse. "Dig in, boy, dig in."

The horse strained against the heavy pull of the rope, and the cow's head turned. It began to swim with all four legs churning underwater, following the rope that was pulling at its horns.

Carey set the brake on the chuck wagon and jumped down to help control the cattle that were trying to put distance between them and the infant rattlers. He waved his hat and turned several back into the herd. Other hands rode up and began to cut cattle out of one bunch and drive them into another.

Roy and Ralph chased down six head and turned them back, pushed them farther up the line away from the place where some of the cattle had disturbed the nest of snakes.

Miles got his cow out of the water and slipped the rope over its boss. The cow shook like a wet dog and splashed water on Abe and Miles, then lumbered off toward the other cattle drifting along the bank.

"Let's get these cattle separated from the snakes," Miles called out as a pair of rattlers slithered past him, streaking through the grass like wriggling darning needles, their rattles setting up a burr of unnerving sound that rippled like electricity up his spine.

Roy and Jules herded the last of the frightened cattle away from the riverbank and drove them into the lumbering herd. Randy's horse reared up and stomped a coiled snake, smashing it to pieces with iron hooves. The horse snorted and sidled away, its eyes fixed on the writhing snake with its bloody innards showing, its head smashed flat.

"Good boy," Randy said, and sat, holding his horse in check as he panted for a decent breath.

Jules rode up to Miles. "You want me to hold the herd a while longer, until Dale gets back?"

"No, Jules. Dale won't be back until sundown. That farm, if that's what it is, is a good ten or twelve miles off. We'll move slow until we get Dale's report."

"I got you, boss," Jules said, and rode off, back to the head of the herd.

Randy rode over, his shirt soaked with sweat, his face clogged with dust.

"Well, we didn't lose any, Miles," he said.

"You did a good job, Randy. All of the hands did."

"You throw a pretty fair loop yourself, Miles."

"Lucky."

"Lucky is where practice gets you," Randy said. "I seen you many a time at roundup hitting your mark with the loop."

"Pa taught me all I know," Miles said. "God bless him."

He wished that Doc was with them that day. His nerves, he decided, were plumb shot. His veins sizzled with energy brought on by the excitement. He felt a warmth in his neck and on his face. His blood must have been racing all through his body. He was tired, but exhilarated. He felt alive and it was as if he could feel every muscle and bone in his body tingling with excitement.

It was then that he turned to look at the sky beyond the river. To the southwest, far off, he saw the darkening sky.

Roy rode up and halted his horse. "You see it too, eh, Miles?"

"That's a gulf storm buildin'," Miles said.

"That's where the big ones come from, sure as fire burns."

"We may be in for it tonight, or maybe tomorrow."

"Them clouds ain't movin' fast from what I've seen. Tomorrow, maybe."

"Early."

"Early maybe. Hard to tell."

"I don't like it none," Miles said. "We got no shelter, nothing to stop the wind or the rain."

"Or a twister," Roy said.

"Don't say that word," Miles said. "Especially not in flat Kansas."

Roy suppressed a laugh. Miles was serious. A tornado could raise hell with a herd. If one ever hit them, they would all be chasing cows until June.

He rode away and started hooing at the cattle, waving his hat.

The herd was moving again, peeling away from the river like ranks of marching beasts, returning to the trail, their curly white faces lit by sunlight, their amber hides glistening with a rippling radiance of reds and oranges, their horns bristling like curved lances, a veritable army of cattle marching off to another engagement, perhaps another battle.

The cattle waded through dancing mirages, pools of water that evaporated into thin air only to reappear again off to the east or, like ghostly mirrors, in the uncharted north.

CHAPTER 20

Pete stood hipshot at the watering trough, neck bent, floppy ears laid back, twitching at the flies gorging on the tender lining. Clarence slipped a feed bag over his mouth and the mule munched on dried oats grown in one of his master's fields.

Clarence looked to the south and saw that the small cloud of dust had disappeared. But, to the southwest, the sky was still ominous, dark with clouds so far away they appeared to be black smudges on the otherwise blue sky with its clumps of cottony clouds suspended in the breezeless atmosphere.

He hooked up the plow after Pete was finished with the oats, hung the canvas bag on the post. He plowed row after row, unearthing a few rocks that had strayed there from a year of rains, and churning up old dead cornstalks that had rotted to desiccated shreds.

186

When the sun stood at what Clarence estimated to be around four o'clock in the afternoon, Clarence saw Floybel returning in the sulky. Dust spooled out from the two wheels and hung in the still air like dirt flung against damp glass. There was just no air stirring that warm afternoon. He had two more rows to plow. He waved to Floybel and she waved back. He saw no more of her until he drove the plow along the edge of the road, floating the blade above the plowed furrows. Pete walked at a good brisk pace all the way to the barn. Floybel was waiting and he could see that she was anxious to talk.

He unhitched the plow and led Pete to a stall in the barn. He gave him water and grain, closed the door, and walked back outside.

Floybel stood in the shade of the barn, tapping her foot on dry ground.

"Jerry Bickham ain't comin'," she said, spitting out the words as if they were bitter bile in her mouth.

"He say why?"

"Yep, he sure did. He said he didn't want no part of tanglin' with Texicans ever again. And none of the other neighbors will come over neither."

"That's a hell of a note," Clarence said.

"Jerry said we got too much land as it is, and he don't have near as much. He said we ought to build a big old road through the middle of it and just charge a toll tax on them herds when they come up."

"I got a road through the middle of the property," Clarence said. He pointed to the road that knifed through all his fields on that side of the river.

"But you don't have no gate and you ain't levyin' taxes to them cowboys what want to cross our land."

They walked up to the house together. Clarence pulled a large bandanna from his back pocket and wiped the grime and sweat off his face. They went to the well and she stood by as he splashed his face and scrubbed his hands with lye soap. She handed him the towel that hung on the hay hook. He dried his hands and face.

"Look yonder," she said, pointing to a place beyond their fields. "I seen him gawkin' and cranin' his neck the whole time I was in that buggy in sight of the house. He's been ridin' up and down for a mile or two, a-lookin' at our land."

Clarence saw the horseman. The man had stopped and was shading his eyes with his hands. He wore the kind of hat he'd seen Texas cattlemen wear and there was a rifle stock sticking up out of its boot. He wore a gun belt and the sun glanced off the cartridges, making them gleam like polished brass ornaments.

"You ought to walk out there and hail him, Clarence. See what he's up to."

"I can do that, I reckon."

"Better take your scattergun with you."

"Now, that wouldn't look too friendly, would it?"

"No, but he's got a rifle and pistol and might just shoot you."

Clarence considered what Floybel said to him. The rider had started moving again, riding alongside the fields that stretched to the east, the fields where milo, corn, and wheat were already better than ankle high.

There were a number of other, smaller farms beyond Clarence's property. They stretched for miles and, he knew, were all planted and prosperous that spring. The ground in that section of Kansas was fertile and homesteads dotted the landscape. Some of the farmers had been there before the war and most of them had come out from Oklahoma, Tennessee, and Kentucky when wild Indians still roamed the land. They had fought for the dirt where they had built their homes, dug and planted and raised families that had spread out clear to Nebraska and beyond. Those men and women had weathered storms and prairie fires, floods, and tornadoes to grow crops that fed people whose fingernails had never been clogged with dirt.

"If he's scoutin' for a trail drive," Clarence said, "he ain't goin' to find no good place 'ceptin' mine." His voice was soft as if he were musing to himself. But Floybel heard every word and she tugged at his arm.

"Go get your scattergun and talk to that feller," she said. "Find out what he's up to. Maybe . . ."

Her voice faded to a silence as the rider turned and rode to the south. That's when they both saw the dust in the sky.

"There it is again," Clarence said.

"I see it," Floybel said. "That's a herd of cattle, sure as rain is wet. And that cowboy is ridin' straight toward it."

"No way I could catch up to him. That ground is rough and would tear the buggy to pieces."

"He'll likely be back tomorrow with a whole bunch of cows a-follerin' him."

"So, Jerry won't come, you say. That's a fine friend for you."

"Nope. None of 'em. They want to keep their skins."

"Well, we'll just have to make do. See if

we can talk them cowboys into crossin' somebody else's land."

They walked back into the house as the sun crawled down the sky toward the western horizon. They both took one last look at the distant black clouds and shook their heads.

Inside, Floybel went to her room to change clothes.

"I'll have supper ready by sundown," she called to Clarence, who stood by the window, staring outside at the dust and the storm clouds spreading across the sky like oil on a lake.

He wondered what a hard rain would do to his young stands of corn, milo, and wheat. To Floybel's garden. They had weathered strong, straight-line winds many times before, and they had both seen twisters and dust devils dance across the land like demon dervishes, whipping up dirt and dust, blasting their faces with grit, scouring the paint off the house and outbuildings. But none of the twisters had made a direct hit on their home or their barns.

In the past, they had seen neighbors come out of storm cellars to see their homes flattened or sailed miles away like toy dollhouses. They had heard the little children screaming, terrified at what had happened to them. They had seen farmers standing on rooftops when the rivers flooded, waving for someone to rescue them from certain death by drowning.

It was a hard land, sometimes, Clarence thought. And sometimes the land took back all that man had constructed upon it, wiped homes and families off its face as if they were of no consequence. People praised God in good times and cursed Him in bad. Some would say that God had saved them, while others wondered why God had been so cruel and heartless to them.

And, some said, everything happened according to some divine mysterious plan that only God knew.

Clarence and Floybel had witnessed many tragedies, and while she read the Bible at night, Clarence studied the stars, the constellations, the moon, and the planets in the night sky. He believed that there was a great force in the universe and that there was a superior being who had created such magnificence. But he didn't hold with people who either praised or blamed God for everything that happened to them.

This was a small bone of contention between him and Floybel, and it had continued after they had lost both their boys. Floybel wondered why God had taken them when they were both so young.

"God didn't take 'em nowhere," Clarence said. "They was kilt, pure and simple."

"Oh, Clarence, you're such a heathen."

"Well, maybe I am a heathen. God made us in all shapes and sizes. He made you a believer. He made me a heathen."

Floybel would laugh at that, and they would go on as they had, both dedicated to their individual beliefs.

After the boys were buried, neither of them ever spoke of an afterlife again.

That was just too big a mystery for both of them.

He heard Floybel clattering about in the kitchen, and he stepped away from the window. He looked at the old musket over the fireplace and the double-barreled shotgun in the glass cabinet where he hung his old Remington .44 converted from cap n' ball to percussion.

He had never used any of those weapons on a man.

And he hoped he never would.

But they were tools like those he kept out in the barn. Someday, he thought, he might have to use them. And it wouldn't be God's will, he knew.

It would be his will.

CHAPTER 21

It was close to sunset when Dale rode back to the herd. The herd was moving along the river. The cattle were not dragging their feet, but they looked tired and ready to bed down. He waved at the outriders and reined up when he saw Miles and Roy on drag, bringing up the rear.

The sky to the west began to take on a gray cast. Blue and purple clouds hung like long loaves of moldy bread above the horizon, and there, off to the southwest, was that growing black mass that seemed to hover in the heavens like some crouching dark behemoth, ready to pounce, its loins girded for war, its haunches coiled to spring. The air was still and it seemed as if the entire prairie had paused and was holding its breath.

"Hey, Miles," Dale said, in a somewhat casual tone, "I hope you ain't in no hurry come morning."

"Why is that?" Miles asked as Dale's horse snorted and bobbed its head up and down as if trying to shake bit and bridle.

"They ain't nothin' but farms yonder. Miles and miles of farms, all of 'em sprouting corn and milo, wheat and hay."

"Where does the trail go?" Roy asked.

"It just plumb peters out," Dale said. "Like it run up against a big ol' wall."

"You sure?" Miles said.

"They's a little old road acrost one farm, but it ain't no cattle trail."

"Shit," Roy said.

"Ditto," Miles echoed.

"How far did you ride east and west?" Roy asked.

"I must've rid three or more miles in both directions. Ain't nothing but farmland far as I could see in either direction."

Dale looked at Miles, a questioning arch to his eyebrows.

"Five extry miles wouldn't hurt us none," Miles said. But it was obvious to Dale and Roy that he wasn't sure.

"If that's all it is," Roy said. "Dale, did you see any sign of a cattle trail? Anywhere?"

Dale shook his head. "If there was a cattle trail, even a skinny one, Roy, I'd've seen it. It's like somebody took a great big broom and swept all signs of a trail away. Not only that, but the main farm I seen, the big one, has posts stuck up for a good stretch."

"Posts?" Miles asked.

"Yep, round old posts like you would stick up in a pole corral. Only these are made of iron or tin or somethin'."

"Posts," Roy said.

"Yep, posts," Dale said. "And them posts got signs tacked to 'em. Big old painted signs."

"Spit it out, Dale," Miles said, plainly irritated. "What in hell did the signs say?"

"Ever' one of 'em said 'Texans Go Home.' In big letters and that warn't all."

"Damn, Roy," Miles said as he looked at Roy, "it's like pullin' teeth from a hippopotamus to get anything out of this man."

"He don't say much, Miles," Dale said, "but he's got a kind face."

"Yeah, the kind I'd like to smash with my fist," Miles said. "Damn it, Dale, what else?"

"Skulls," Dale said, and let the word float over the other two men like some ancient scrap of parchment. Dale's eyes glittered in the dying light of the day, and he wet his lips with his tongue as the word seemed to sink in with his two listeners.

Cattle lowed and kept moving like some lumbering aggregation of curly-haired beasts on a pilgrimage to a slaughterhouse.

"Skulls?" Miles asked. "Human skulls?"

"Nope. Cattle skulls," Dale said.

"Cattle skulls?" Roy repeated in disbelief.

"All bone and white, with empty eye sockets, and bleached horns, like they was dipped in acid to burn the hide off."

"Shit," Miles said.

"Gave me the pure willies," Dale said.

The men walked their horses behind the herd as the western sky began to fade into a deeper gray and the blue over the horizon faded like chambray after many washings in lye soap.

They did not speak for several moments.

Then Dale said, "Well, shoot. It looks like Farmer Brown is expectin' us."

"We have to get this herd through," Miles said, a stubborn bone in his teeth. "Maybe we can bargain with one of them farmers."

"Them boiled skulls tell a sorry tale, boss," Dale said.

"If that farmer or any of 'em shoots one of my cows, I'll run right over him," Miles said.

"That's the spirit, Miles," Roy said. "Farmer Brown murders a cow, you murder him."

"I didn't mean it that way, Roy. I meant we got to get these cattle up to Salina, farm or no farm."

"Well, you got all night to think about it," Roy said. "It's goin' to be pitch-dark and them clouds will block off any light from the moon."

Miles looked off to the west. The blackness was creeping across the sky and he saw the silver glitter of the evening star in the pale border that still held a trace of blue.

"Bed 'em down, Roy," Miles said. "Dale, you tell Jules to bunch 'em up. We'll camp here for the night."

"We might have to beat a storm that's raggin' our tail," Roy said. "From the looks of that sky to the southwest."

"Maybe Farmer Brown won't see us if we get a heavy rain," Miles said as they both watched Dale ride off toward the head of the herd.

"You do have a sense of humor, Miles. Otherwise, I couldn't live with you."

Miles laughed a dry mirthless laugh and both men crowded in on the rumps of the cattle in the rear, pushing them until the herd seemed to stop all up and down the line, as if on cue.

Miles turned and waved to Carey, beckoning for him to pull wide of the herd and set up night camp. Carey turned the horses and flanked the herd as the night came on in a sudden rush, the sky filled with stars and the Milky Way sprawled across the sky in a wide band of sparkling diamonds.

The herd settled down. Some of the cattle bent their knees and slumped to the earth. Others followed as riders circled them, singing "Oh! Susanna" and "The Camptown Races" in low tones. Carey had the cook fire blazing and the smell of food wafted on the still night air. When he banged the metal triangle, some of the men rode up and dismounted, dusting themselves off with hand pats and hat slaps. They got their plates and eating utensils, stood in a line as Carey dished boiled beef and turnips onto their plates and pointed to a basket of yesterday's biscuits and a bottle of ketchup next to the salt and pepper shakers.

"I'll take the morning watch," Miles said after supper.

"You don't have to," Jules said. "I'll be up come midnight."

"I don't think I can sleep," Miles said. "Thinkin' about tomorrow."

"Hell, Miles, don't let them farmers put a burr under your blanket," Roy said. "Way I figger it, they're already housebroke."

"What do you mean?" Miles asked, vapors of coffee floating up from the cup in his hand so that his lips were moist.

"If they got signs up 'gainst Texans, means

they already had run-ins with a herd or two. My bet is them other Texans got through one way or another. They might have lost a cow or two, but they got to the railhead."

"I think Roy's right," Randy said. "No farmer can stop a big old herd from crossin' his land. I mean, ain't that illegal? Like restraint of trade or somethin' like that?"

"Boy, you been readin' too many of them Dallas papers," Jules said. "A man's got a right to pertect his property."

"Sure," Randy said, "but if'n the govamint wants your land, they can take it, 'thout nobody sayin' nothin'. It's Eminent Domain."

"He does read, don't he?" Dale said, flicking the ash from his cigarette into the fire. "Govamint's one thing, cattlemen's another, I say."

"Well, we might have the law on our side," Randy said, but his words were crippled and lame and they died on the ears of the others, some of whom snorted at him in dismissal.

"We won't solve it at this campfire," Miles said. "That's for sure. We'll see what Farmer Brown has to say come mornin'. If he has a bunch of others backin' him up, we might have to drive east for a long ways."

"Yeah, we might have to make a big old

circle and come into Salina from New York," Carey cracked as he scraped a plate into the fire.

Ralph Beasely wandered into the fire circle on foot. The others looked up at the fiftyish man who was still one of the tougher men on the drive. They could almost hear his bones creak. They certainly heard his knees crackle when he sat down and asked Carey for a cup of coffee.

"Cattle ain't restless tonight," he said. "Like they know we're goin' to run into trouble in the mornin'."

Carey poured Ralph a cup of coffee in a tin cup.

"You think cows can see into the future, Beasely?" Dale asked.

"They sure as hell know when a storm's a-comin'. Dogs too. And horses."

"Oh yeah?" Randy said. "Cows are dumber'n dogs or horses. They don't know their asses from their noses."

"All the same," Ralph said as he blew steam off his coffee, "these cattle are sure restin' up."

The talk continued until men got up and walked to their horses to ride nighthawk or crawl onto their bedrolls for some shut-eye. Miles was the last to leave the fire.

"You want me to give you a couple of

toothpicks, boss?" Carey asked him when he took his empty cup.

"What for?"

"So's you can keep your eyes open. You ain't had no sleep and you're nighthawkin'."

"Coffee'll keep me awake, Carey. Don't you worry none."

"G'night, Miles."

"Good night, Carey."

Miles found his horse and climbed into the saddle. He rode in a slow loop around the herd. Some of the cattle were still grazing, but most were bedded down. Some chewed their cuds and moaned at his passing. One or two flicked a tail as if to swat mosquitoes or flies.

CHAPTER 22

The storm struck with a vengeance just before dawn. The cowhands were all awake and they had the herd moving when wind and rain whipped across the prairie. Thunder boomed; lightning flashed all around them like some demonic fireworks show. Men yelled and cattle bellowed. Yellow slickers bobbed in the predawn dark like lit lanterns. The river churned with raindrops and waves smacked against the banks and rolled frothy combers in all directions.

The rain invigorated Miles, who was still bleary-eyed from lack of sleep. But he had enjoyed riding around the herd and helping out when Jules got the cattle up and headed north.

"Better send Dale back out to scout," Miles said.

"Dale is ridin' flank. I sent Randy on up ahead. I figger we won't run into any farms for another five or six miles."

"We must have covered five mile already," Miles said.

"Yep, at least. Cattle are runnin' away from that storm. They don't know no better."

"You tell that to Ralph, Jules."

Jules laughed and turned his horse. He rode to the head of the herd while Miles rode to the rear.

Roy was riding back and forth, urging the cattle in the rear to keep forging forward.

"Hell of a storm," Roy said.

"If it moves fast, it won't bother us much. We'll know more when it gets light."

"When's that gonna be?" Roy cracked, and Miles laughed as he managed the right rear flank.

It did get light.

But it was a peculiar light, yellowish and gray in the east, purple and gray to the west. The light kept shifting, wallowing through shredded clouds, changing colors. Some of the black clouds were high, but the lower clouds dripped gray tendrils that were rain, and the wind swirled around them, circling like some sniffing wolf.

"I don't like this none," Roy said. "Look at that sky back there, Miles."

Miles looked back. The sky was almost colorless under the clouds, but it had a deathly pall to it and some of the clouds kept dipping down like probing fingers, only to pull back up as if testing the land or pushed by the fickle winds.

Randy rode up three hours later, out of breath, his face shiny with rain, his hat dripping water from its brim.

"Miles, you better come up," he gasped. "Jules is haltin' the herd."

"What's up?" Miles asked.

"I run into that farm and they's a man and woman standin' out there under a parasol like they was a-goin' to Sunday meetin'."

"I'll be right there," Miles said.

"Want me to go with you?" Roy asked.

"Yeah. Randy, you stay here. Rest yourself."

"Thanks, boss," Randy said. And as Roy and Miles started to ride off, he said: "Oh, I think that farmer and his wife are totin' firearms."

Jules was waiting for them. He had the herd stopped in front of the posts with warning signs on them, and the skulls of dead cattle. It was an eerie scene in the rain and wind. On the small road that dissected the farm, Miles saw a man and woman, both wearing dark slickers, standing with an open umbrella over their heads.

Both of them held on to the umbrella's handle, but it was like holding on to a tiger's tail. The wind whipped at them and the umbrella rose and fell with every gust.

"They were just standin' there," Jules told Miles. "They ain't said a word, nor been threatenin'. But I think the farmer's got him a Greener under his coat, and the woman, I think she's got a pistol in that black bag she's totin'."

"I'll go over and talk to them. You keep the men back. I don't want to start a gunfight here."

"No, sir. Me neither. But we can't just run our cattle up that road with them two a-standin' there."

"No, Jules, we can't," Miles said in a calm voice.

"Want me to go with you, Miles?" Roy asked.

"No, you stay here with Jules. I'm going to walk over."

Miles reached under his slicker and began to unbuckle his gun belt.

"You ain't gonna walk over there unarmed, are you?" Roy asked.

"Yeah, I am." He buckled the belt and handed it to Jules. "Keep it dry if you can," he said. He dismounted and handed the reins of his horse to Roy.

206

"Wish me luck," he said to both men.

Miles walked toward the Ruggleses. He tried to avoid puddles, mainly to prove that he wasn't hostile, that he came in peace. He did not look at the two people as he walked toward them. He didn't want to appear threatening in any way.

"Good morning," Miles said as he stopped up to the couple. "Ma'am. Sir. I'm Miles Blaine from Dumas, Texas."

"We know you're from Texas," Clarence said. "And them cows ain't goin' to tramp down my crops."

"And what is your name, sir?" Miles asked.

"Clarence. Clarence Ruggles."

"And you, ma'am? You're Mrs. Ruggles?"

"I'm Floybel Ruggles," she said. "Clarence is my husband. We own this farm you're aimin' to cross."

"Well, there just isn't any other place we can go," Miles said. "You got a road there. We can drive the cattle in small thin bunches right up that road and we won't tromp down any of your crops."

"That's what you say," Clarence said.

"That's what I mean, Clarence. We don't aim to cause any damage to your farm. We only have less'n three thousand head and my hands are real experienced. If that road goes plumb across your land, we'll stay on it and get out of your hair as quick as possible."

Clarence and Floybel looked at each other. She shook her head.

"Nope," Clarence said, "it's just too risky."

Then Miles saw both people stand up straight and stare at the sky behind him. He turned and saw what they had just seen.

At the same time, he heard his men yelling. And the cattle were kicking up a rumpus as well.

A huge black cloud had dropped low over the land and a large funnel was just touching the ground.

Miles gasped. His mouth gaped open.

"That's a twister, by God," Clarence yelled. "And it's comin' right at us."

The tornado bellowed like a hundred trains and roamed the land in a crooked walk with that pointed finger dredging up grass and earth and flinging pieces of wood brush.

The umbrella flew out of Clarence's and Floybel's hands and sailed toward the house and barn.

"Clarence," Floybel screamed. "It's headin' right for our house."

"God A'mighty," Clarence said.

Miles saw that the twister was going to

cut a wide swath on the other side of the river and probably smash the farmer's house and barns to smithereens. He acted fast, grabbing Clarence by his collar and reaching for Floybel. His shotgun dropped to the ground. Floybel hung on to her purse with both hands.

"Come with me," he yelled above the terrible din of the tornado.

Blindly, they followed him. He pushed them both toward the river, then hurled them down to the ground, flat on their faces. He fell on them both and pinned them down.

The roar of the twister drowned out all other sound. It swept across the land in a fury, whirling like some gyrating machine. As they watched, it smashed into the two-story home and lifted it into the air. Pieces of lumber flew in all directions. Then the tornado continued its path of destruction and flailed into one barn, then another. Horses, the mule, and two Guernsey milk cows flew through the air and landed hard. Floybel screamed. Clarence began to sob.

It was over in mere minutes.

The twister weaved on and then its funnel lifted from the ground and disappeared in the folds of the cloud that had spawned it.

Miles helped Clarence and Floybel to

their feet.

They both looked at him with sad eyes.

"Mister, I think you done saved our lives," Clarence said. "Let me shake your hand."

"Oh, Clarence," Floybel said, "look what happened. There ain't nothin' left. Our home is gone."

Clarence put his arms around his wife and drew her close.

"We ain't lost everything," he said. "We got ourselves and . . ."

She looked at Miles and nodded.

"You saved us," she said. "If you hadn't run us over here, we'd have been blown plumb away."

Miles looked at the road. All of the posts and the signs and the skulls were no longer there.

"Mr. Miles," Clarence said. "You take your cattle up that road and get on to where you're goin'."

"Thanks, Clarence. We'll take it slow and my cattle won't eat your corn or tear up your fields, if there's anything left."

"That's good enough for me," Clarence said, and offered his hand.

Miles shook it, then turned to where Jules and Roy were hunkered down under their horses' bellies.

"A few head at a time," Miles called out.

"Keep 'em on that road."

Both men grinned.

There were no more twisters that day, and by the time Miles reached the end of the Ruggles farm road, there was nothing but open prairie ahead.

And the cattle sogged over rain-saturated ground, looking like a bunch of oversized hamsters, soaked to their pink Hereford skins.

CHAPTER 23

Miles kept the herd to the east of the Arkansas River after he and his men turned the herd north. He knew, from his map, that he still had to cross the Little Arkansas. They had left the Cimarron four days ago. The cattle had plenty of grass and good drinking water, so he knew they were faring well.

"If we can keep the herd going at this pace," Miles said to Tad Rankin, "we'll beat that deadline by a country mile."

"I figger we can cross the fork at Great Bend," Rankin said. "Then we'll have a clear shot to Salina."

"So far, so good."

"Except I think we got a man follerin' us. He was just a dot when I first caught sight of him, but he's gainin' on us."

Miles turned around in the saddle. The sky was blue and the land was green as far as he could see. Some prairie swifts hurtled past him and his gaze followed them until they disappeared.

"I don't see nothin'," Miles said.

"He ain't close to the riverbank, Miles," Tad said. "Look yonder about ten degrees left and you'll see him."

"Is he close or far?" Miles strained to see where Tad pointed with his outstretched arm and hand, but the heat waves shimmered off the prairie grass and he only saw watery blurs.

"You got to look down low, then let him ride into your eyesight. An old trick I learned scoutin' for Custer."

Miles did what Tad had told him and held his gaze steady as the herd moved on away from them, the cows snatching grass every few yards as they lumbered in a long, wide phalanx behind the leaders far up ahead.

He heard the drumming boom of a prairie chicken in the distance, and doves flew along the river like winged gray darts, their wings whistling as they carved the air in their flight path.

"I see a tiny dot," Miles said, shielding his eyes under the brim of his hat. "Wait, yes, it's moving. I can't tell if it's a man on horseback or a buffalo."

"It ain't no buffalo," Tad said with a grin. "Just keep lookin'. The longer we sit here, the closer he's going to get."

"All right."

"I been watchin' him. He'll walk his horse for a stretch, then gallop, then slow down. He looks like a man who's in a mighty hurry to catch up with us."

"Oh yeah. He's got the horse in a dead run now. I can see the man. Hard to make out his horse, though."

"You want to wait here for him, see what he wants, or just keep ridin' drag till he catches up with us?"

Miles looked at the rear end of the herd. The cattle were now at least two or three hundred yards away and some of those in the rear were stopping to eat grass and a few were straying from the pack.

"I reckon we'll have to chase down strays if we don't get back on drag," Miles said.

"If you can handle it, I'll stay here and ride out to meet him."

"You think he's chasin' after us, Tad?"

"That rider. He's got him a purpose or he wouldn't be pushin' his horse that hard in this heat."

"Whatever you think is best," Miles said.

"I'll linger here awhile longer. We got all day. When he gets close enough, I'll wave to him."

"Wave to him?" Miles looked puzzled.

"If he waves back, I'll know he's wantin' to catch up with us."

"Who in hell could it be? I wonder."

"It's either a farmer who's got a sick cow or a cowhand lookin' for work."

"Or a rancher wantin' us to get off his land," Miles said, and turned his horse. "Let me know what you find out."

"Sure thing, Miles. That one cow at the rear wants to stay in one spot and eat. You better show her who's boss."

Both men laughed as Miles rode off to catch up with the herd, which was looking like a bunch of droopy-drawered kids walking home from school.

Tad dug out the makings from his pocket and rolled a quirly. He lit it and drew the blue smoke into his lungs. He blew out a plume of smoke and watched it float away and become cobwebs as the river breeze snatched its curls and scissored them to shreds.

The rider drew closer, but was still more than two miles away, perhaps less. It was difficult to judge distances with the pools of mirages forming on the bare spots near the horizon. At times, it seemed that the rider was wading through a small lake or a pond, and the legs of the horse quivered in the gauzy light. They were into May and Kansas

215

was already hot with summer more than a month away. There were no trees for protection. The land was flat as far as he could see in any direction, and the sun high overhead blazed down on man and beast without a cloud to block its searing rays.

When the rider was close enough, less than a mile away, Tad put out his cigarette and looked closely at the horse. There was something familiar about it. The man was bobbing up and down and it was difficult to see what he was wearing. But the shape of his hat looked somewhat familiar as well.

Another quarter mile closer and Tad raised a hand in greeting. He gave a slow wig-wag with his arm, as if he were communicating in semaphore. The man raised his hand and waved.

Tad rode out to meet him. When he looked over his shoulder, he could longer see the herd. There was only a thin scrim of dust to mark its progress, so faint he could barely see it.

"Tad, is that you?" the man called.

Tad squinted. "Norm? Norm Collins?"

Norm rode up and the two men slapped open palms.

"You come a fur piece, Norm," Tad said. "I reckon you got a good reason."

"You were easy to track," Norm said, his

face cracking open in a wide grin.

"Well, you're a tracker, I know."

"I been burnin' daylight and moonlight both, Tad. I got to see Miles."

"Well, he's ridin' drag. Somethin' important?"

"Real important."

"What is it?"

"I'd better just tell Miles what I come to tell him. No offense. It's personal."

"All right."

The two men rode at a steady walk. There was some lather on the chest of Norm's horse, a few streaks where flies supped. The horse's chest jiggled to shake them off, but the winged feeders persisted.

"I can tell you one thing, though, that might interest you, Tad."

"Yeah? What's that?"

"Miles too will be mighty interested."

"Let's hear it," Tad said.

"You got another herd on your tail. Better'n a thousand head, about three days back. And the drovers are pushin' it pretty hard."

"Another herd? Following our track?"

"Just a-steppin' into your same tracks."

"Hmm. Wonder where they come from."

"I know where they come from. It's Miles's brother, Jared."

"Jared Blaine?"

"You catch on real quick, Tad. Yep, Jared's runnin' not only Lazy J stock, but, mixed in, I saw some Slash B cattle."

"Jumpin' Jehosephat."

"Yeah, that's what I thought. I ain't seen Doc, but I knowed he was up to Perryton 'cause Ethyl told me where he'd gone."

"What was you doin' at Ethyl's?"

"I'll say no more, Tad, until I talk to Miles."

"Well, shoot, Norm. I could die of curiosity any dadgummed minute."

Norm smiled, but went silent.

The two men caught up with Miles, who turned and saw them. He, like Tad, was surprised to see Norm.

"You think I need another hand, Norm?" Miles said when he got close.

"Nope, but I got to talk to you, Miles. Can you let Tad ride drag for a few minutes? It's important."

"Sure, Tad's going to go to the head of the line pretty quick. What brings you all the way up to Kansas?"

Tad rode away and Norm waited until he was out of earshot.

"Miles, I got bad news for you. Reason I rode like hell to catch up to you."

"Is Ethyl all right?"

"It ain't Ethyl. It's your wife, Caroline."

"Caroline? What's wrong with her."

Norm told him the entire story. While he was talking, he knew that Miles was getting sick. By the time he was finished telling him about Rawson and how he had nearly killed Caroline, Miles had leaned over and vomited what was left of his breakfast and most of his lunch. When he recovered, his face was drenched with sweat and all the blood had fled from his visage.

"Is she going to live?" Miles asked as the two started riding toward the herd.

"I reckon, but she's plumb addled, Miles. She can't put two words together and I don't think she knows who Ethyl is anymore. You look at her eyes and there ain't nothin' in 'em."

"I'll kill that little son of a bitch," Miles said.

"By now, Doc must be back from Perryton and him and Ethyl will do what they can for your wife."

"What was my pa doin' up in Perryton?"

"You might as well hear the rest of it, Miles. I think Doc's got more'n one ace up his sleeve."

"You'd better put that in plain English, Norm."

Norm told him about Jared's herd, hot on

their heels. Heading for the same railhead, he figured.

"Well, I'll be damned," Miles said. "You got any good news, Norm?"

"You got yourself an extry hand."

"Maybe I ought to ride back home and see what I can do for poor Caroline."

"You'll see your pa in Salina, Miles. He'd want you to bring this herd there."

"Yeah. And I sure want to talk to Jared when we meet up."

"You may not have long to wait on that. He was three or so days behind you, but I reckon by the time we get to the Little Arkansas or maybe Great Bend, he'll be in your back pocket."

"Another two or three days, maybe."

"Maybe," Norm said.

They caught up to the herd as the sun dipped lower in the western sky. Miles was silent for a long time and then he told Tad about Caroline.

"I'm real sorry, Miles. I never liked that Rawson kid."

"I could kill myself for hiring him."

"You can't cry over spilt milk, Miles," Tad said. "A kid like that will do it to someone else. If he's got a problem with the Barleycorn, he won't do much and likely's goin' to have a short life."

"If I ever see him again, his life will be real short," Miles said.

He gritted his teeth and tried not to cry, but the tears squeezed out anyway. He thought about Caroline and Jared, his ma and pa. Everything seemed to be crashing down on him and he had nowhere to turn. He couldn't go back home. He had a herd to drive and a deadline to make.

What was it his pa had told him a long time ago?

He remembered it now.

"Fix the things you can and let the rest go hang, son. Otherwise you'll worry yourself into an early grave."

Miles drew a deep breath and wiped the tears from his cheeks. He said a silent "thanks" to Doc, his father, and the sky glowed like the stained glass windows in a cathedral, with all the colors of the rainbow painted on clouds and the distant horizon.

CHAPTER 24

The pace Jared had set was brutal for men, cattle, and horses. But the drive was gobbling up nearly twenty miles a day, and the days were long. Jared did not bed the herd down until long after sundown and he had the herd moving well before sunup.

"You're pushing the herd pretty hard, Jared," Roy said one morning when cows and horses were still stumbling through the dark, the Arkansas a slate ribbon glistening past with stars in its ripples.

"You don't like it, Roy, you can ride back to the Slash B," Jared retorted, his ire rising to the surface like the first bubble in a pot of boiling water.

"Hey, don't be so damned touchy, Jared. I ain't a quitter and I take anything throwed at me, hard or soft."

"Well, you ain't the only hand gripin' about the pace. Some of the others are startin' to look like mutineers."

"We're makin' good time. If it's the deadline you're worried about, forget it. We'll beat June first by a week at least."

"It ain't the damned deadline, Roy. It's Miles. I want to beat him to Salina and it's plain that's where he's headed. I get sick just lookin' at his tracks."

"Hard to make up two days in this heat," Roy said.

"Cattle are not losin' weight that I can see, and there's grass and water all the way."

"Some of the cattle are losing weight, Jared. This keeps up, you'll be drivin' skeletons to the railhead."

Jared laughed wryly. He chased a cow back into the herd that had wandered off-track, and then he returned to riding drag with Roy.

"We get paid by the head, not the pound, Roy," he said.

"But you know Doc wants to make a good impression on the buyer. He's thinkin' about next spring, not just this one measly little drive."

"We'll do all right. I just want to see my brother's face when I ride up on his sorry ass."

Roy kept silent, but later that day, when they were stopped for a quick bite of grub at noon, he heard Jared talking to Paco.

"I want you to send one of the men up ahead to scout Miles's herd."

"I can do that, Jared," Paco said. "But why?"

"I want to know just how far ahead of us he is."

"You'll be takin' a man out for three, maybe four days, round-trip."

"We can handle it," Jared said. "The herd's as tame as Granny's house cat by now."

"Yeah, the herd's doin' just fine," Paco said. "As long as the weather holds and we don't get a Kansas twister, or run across a bunch of angry farmers, and it don't rain. . . ."

"I get the point, Paco," Jared said. "Send your best rider and tell him to ride his ass off and come back with the information on where Miles is and how long it's going to take to catch up to him."

Paco chose Will Becker as his scout. Will was the strongest man in the outfit. He had a good strong horse and knew the country. He knew how to avoid trouble, as he had proven when he went to Leavenworth, and he knew how to take care of himself in a fight.

"Jared wants to know how far ahead of us

Miles is, and if we can catch up to him. Can do?"

"I can," Becker said.

"Stock up with grub you can eat in the saddle and get some toothpicks to hold your eyes open. You ain't goin' to sleep on the ground, so you don't need your bedroll. Got it?"

"I got it," Becker said, and rode to the chuck wagon. In moments, he was off at a gallop, heading north along the Canadian.

Roy watched until Becker disappeared and then saw that Jared had been watching him too.

Jared fixed Roy with an icy stare.

"You got something to say, Roy?" Jared demanded.

"Not a thing, Jared," Roy said, and that ended it as far as he was concerned.

Jared meant to beat his brother any way he could, in love or war. It would be suicide, he knew, for any man to come between them in their private and personal fight.

But Roy was filled with a deep sense of dread. If they managed to meet up with Miles, and there was a strong chance that they would, he wanted no part of that quarrel.

For Roy wanted to come back from this strange drive, not only in one piece, but alive and breathing.

It was, he knew, going to be another long, long day, and there would be another long day after that.

He braced himself inwardly, and thought about what Paco told Becker.

He might need some toothpicks himself before this drive was over.

CHAPTER 25

The Rocking M herd stopped dead in its tracks.

Tad Rankin was the first to notice that the herd was no longer moving.

"I wonder what's wrong," Miles said. "Who's riding lead?"

"I put Joadie Lee up there," Tad said.

"What do you think?"

"Well, we ought to be purt near at Great Bend by now. Him and Curly Bob are probably scoutin' for a place to ford."

"I'd better go up and check," Miles said. "You hold the rear, will you?"

"Sure, Miles."

Miles rode off along the length of the stalled cattle.

Tad cocked a leg up and nestled the saddle horn on the underside of his knee. He tipped his hat back slightly and pulled a sack of tobacco from his pocket. He rolled a cigarette, licked it, and stuck it in his mouth. He scratched a match on his boot heel and lit the quirly, drew smoke into his lungs.

It was a fine afternoon, he thought. They had lost some time that morning when some of the cattle got into a nest of rattlesnakes. They burst from the herd like a covey of startled quail and it took him and three other men over an hour to run the snakes off and round up all the strays. Wexler had wanted to shoot the snakes, but Tad held him in check.

"You want to have a full-blown stampede on your hands, Lenny?"

Wexler shook his head and holstered his pistol.

"I always wanted to shoot the head off a rattler," he said.

"Save it for another time, Lenny."

So they had lost a couple of hours, but Tad knew they could make Great Bend that day, regardless. However, he was going by a map, crudely drawn at that, and mileages were uncertain if not downright wrong. He just knew that the Little Arkansas would cross their path and Great Bend was supposed to be the best place to cross. After that, they would have little water and probably not as much grass.

Several minutes later, long after Tad had

finished his cigarette, rolled the butt into a ball, and tossed it to the ground, he saw Miles riding toward him at a fast gallop. The herd grazed and spread out, but so far none had drifted too far from their course.

"We got trouble, Tad," Miles said when he rode up.

"You at the bend?"

"I — I think so, but there's armed men up there. They got rifles and they say we got to pay a toll. I don't know what to do."

"How much toll?" Tad asked.

"Two bits a head."

Tad swore.

"That's if we pay them hard cash right away. If we try and cross somewhere else, they said they'd foller us and we'd have to pay four bits a head."

Tad swore again.

"How many men they got?" he asked.

"I counted twenty. They're a rough-lookin' bunch. The leader's a man named Pete Boggs. There's a ferry there and he says he owns it."

"It's a holdup," Tad said. "Outright robbery."

"I know. I told him we didn't have no money. You know what he said?"

"No, but I guess he didn't like it."

"He said unless we paid, we couldn't

cross. Nowheres."

"So, what are you aimin' to do, Miles?"

"I want you to come up and talk to Boggs. Tell him we'll give him a tally and pay him on the way back."

"Did you tell him that?"

"I just now thought of it," Miles said.

"I'll go up with you and talk to the man," Tad said.

"Let me get someone to hang on to the tails of these cattle."

Tad called to Pedro as they rode near him.

"Pedro, you go back and ride drag," Tad said.

"The herd is not moving," Pedro said.

"Just watch the tail end while I'm gone, will you?"

"Sure, Tad. I will watch their butts if you say so. I ain't doin' nothin' here anyway."

The cattle were lining up at Great Bend, drinking. On the other side of the Little Arkansas, there was a line of men on horseback, all with their rifles pointed skyward, the stocks braced on their legs or pommels. Close to the near shore, a large raft lay at the harbor, ropes tied to wooden posts. A half dozen men leaned against the railings, rifles braced against their legs. They all wore pistols and their cartridge belts bristled with brass bullets.

"That's Boggs there, standing in front of the ferry," Miles whispered to Tad. "The one with the mean face."

"They all got mean faces, Miles," Tad said.

Boggs walked toward them. He was the only man there who was not carrying a rifle. He wasn't tall, nor did he appear muscular. He had a ferret face that was covered with black stubble from chin to mouth. His eyes were small and close-set, and his hat bore grease stains and a few moth holes. He wore coveralls and a gun belt, work boots with large heels as if to make himself taller, but Tad knew they were farmer's shoes and would not slip from stirrups. The man's shirt was a faded blue denim streaked with sweat and he wore a red bandanna around his throat.

"This your foreman?" Boggs asked Miles as he walked up.

"He represents some of the cattle from another ranch," Miles said.

"You boys come up from Texas?"

"We did," Tad said. He climbed out of the saddle and walked up to Pete Boggs. He looked down on Boggs. "I'm Tad Rankin, and I ride for the Slash B brand."

It was plain to see that Boggs wasn't impressed.

"You headin' for Salina, I hear," Boggs said.

"We have a contract to sell our cattle there," Tad said as Miles looked on from the saddle.

"You probably got a deadline too, ain't ye?"

"We do," Tad said.

"Well, we got ourselves a deadline here. Ain't nobody, leastways nobody from Texas, crosses this river without payin' the toll. Two bits a head."

"I think Mr. Blaine here told you that we have no money, Mr. Boggs."

"Then you don't cross with these here cows."

"I have an offer for you, Mr. Boggs," Miles said. "A suggestion."

"Yeah?" Boggs looked up at Miles, squinting in the glare of the sun.

"Yes," Miles said. "You can count our cattle and figure the toll, and we'll surely pay you twenty-five cents a head on our way back home from Salina."

Boggs laughed and turned to the men on the ferry. "Did you hear that, boys? They say they'll pay the toll on their way back home. Should we trust 'em?"

The men on the raft all yelled, "No."

"There you have it, gents," Boggs said.

"We don't trust nobody. In particular, we don't trust Texicans. Now you either pay my toll or you turn right around and go back where you come from."

Boggs fixed his gaze on Tad. He took a straw from his pocket and stuck it in his mouth. He began to chew on it as he waited for an answer from the cattlemen.

"We — we'll have to talk it over," Miles said. "Among ourselves. Give us some time."

"Longer you wait, the higher the toll," Boggs said.

"Why?" Miles asked.

"That's just the way we work it. You ain't the first to try and sell Texas cattle up in Kansas. We're poor farmers. We don't live in big houses and have Negro servants like you folks down south."

"We don't live in big houses and we don't have servants," Miles said.

"Ain't no use arguin' about it, Mr. Blaine. You pay the toll or you don't cross."

"Let's go, Tad," Miles said. "We'll have to figure something out, Mr. Boggs. This is unexpected and, like I said, we don't have that much cash among us."

"Makes no never mind to me, Mr. Blaine. You take all night for all I care. You come talk tomorrow, it's four bits a head, and the day after that, it's six bits, and then a whole dollar. You suit yourself."

With that, Boggs turned and walked back to the ferry. He climbed aboard and ordered his men to untie the ropes and pole them back across the river.

Tad saw the men on horseback watching from the farther bank. They looked like guerilla troops ready to start a war.

Curly Bob, who had been listening, spoke to Tad and Miles.

"It's a damned standoff," he said.

"Curly Bob, you just shut up," Tad said. "We don't need no tempers just yet."

"Sorry, Tad. I just feel like, well, like we can't let a bunch of Kansas sodbusters boss us around and put guns to our heads."

"We'll figure out something, Curly Bob. You just hold tight and keep an eye on this herd. Them jayhawks just might fire off them rifles and start a stampede."

"Yes, sir," Curly Bob said. "I'll keep my damned trap shut."

As Tad rode away with Miles, he looked back at the armed men and the ferry. He didn't count them, but he knew they were outnumbered.

"This could get real ugly," he told Miles when they were alone.

"It already is. What do you think we ought

to do? Find another place to cross?"

"Them jaspers would foller us up- and downriver and we would never get this herd to Salina."

"So, what do we do?"

Tad drew in a breath.

"We may have to fight 'em," he said, somewhat startled at his own words.

There were almost eighteen hundred head of cattle in the herd. He couldn't even figure the toll at two bits a head, but he knew they couldn't pay it. They could only wait and think while Boggs had them by the throat.

One thing Tad knew for sure. The herd could go no farther that day, and might not move by tomorrow.

He didn't see any way out of it. Either they could turn back or they could fight their way across the river.

And if they did that, he knew, the river would run with blood.

CHAPTER 26

Will Becker rode into his second night on the lone trail like a sleepwalker, or in his case, as he thought to himself, a sleep-rider. His horse, a gelding he called "Jock," had begun to stumble and as the night wore on, Becker detected a slight stagger in the animal's gait.

He had dozed only fitfully and now, in the darkness, his mind began playing tricks on him. Every shadow and shape seemed a threat and every sound an alarm in his brain. But Will was a determined man and rode on, a sagging exhausted hulk in a saddle that had become like iron so that his butt was numb and his legs useless appendages that he massaged often to restore circulation in his veins and arteries.

The drone of the frogs along the riverbank lulled him into a stupor until he heard the undertones of crickets sawing their orchestral pieces in an annoying contrapuntal discord. Then mosquitoes boiled up out of the grasses and tide pools, nipped at his cheeks, set off a zinging in his ears as they circled for a blood strike on his jaw. He slapped at them, which only raised welts on his face that made the blood draw even easier for the pesky insects.

These noises and bitings served to keep Becker from dozing off, but his eyelids seemed to grow heavier and it was difficult to keep his eyes open. Jock was just plodding along, swinging legs that were weary and fly-bitten, caked with streaks of dried blood. His hooves barely made a muffled sound on the grass that swished against his long, lean legs.

Earlier, bullbats had cut invisible swaths in the evening sky and now they were gone, taking the dim silver dollars on their wings with them, and only a few small bats plied both banks of the river, lapping up mosquitoes and gnats with unerring accuracy despite their poor eyesight.

Every muscle in Will's body had gone beyond ache and he felt as if all life had gone out of tissue and bone, sinew and muscle. He slapped at insects and drew blood when he made a direct hit. They swarmed around his face, which helped keep him awake. Jock's neck quivered as the hide rippled to shake off the biting insects, and the horse tossed its head and blinked its eyes to escape the swarm of hungry mosquitoes that circled him in plastic black clouds.

In the distance, Becker thought he saw a flicker of light. At first he thought his eyes were deceiving him and that it was only the golden wink of a firefly. Then he smelled cattle and the heady scent of dung. He strained his eyes to see through the darkness. The moon was behind a large cloud and the stars so far away they were merely silvery specks on a velvet tapestry, the Milky Way a blur of dim light that barely illuminated the grass with a patina of pale pewter.

The smells grew stronger and stung his nose with the heady scent of cattle and horses. He rode on, his gaze fixed on the flickering pinpoint of orange light off to his right on the flat expanse of prairie.

He stiffened in the saddle and began to flex his legs and arms. He blinked his eyes to clear his gauzy vision. He slapped at a mosquito with its zinging sound near his right ear and felt a sting in his cheek on the other side.

He was awake, but just barely, and the light grew closer and larger. Then he heard the soft lowing of cattle and knew that he was not dreaming. The pungent aroma of cow pies was stronger in his nostrils and he realized he was riding through masses of fresh cattle and horse droppings.

A few minutes later, Becker heard a low voice humming a vaguely familiar tune. It sounded to him like "Get Along Cindy," but his mind was so addled he couldn't be sure. Then he saw the dim shape of a man on horseback and, beyond, the white faces of cattle as they moved and grazed, their bodies dark and only the ghostly images of their heads visible to him.

"You there," Becker called, and realized his voice was a croak. "Do you see me?"

"I see you," the rider said.

"What herd is this?" Becker asked.

"Not that it's any of your damned business, but it's mostly the Rocking M."

"I'm Will Becker, riding for the Lazy J."

"Well, come on up, Becker. I'm Curly Bob Naylor from down Dumas way."

"Hey, Curly Bob. I'm mighty glad to see you. Is that your campfire yonder?"

"Sure is. Miles is having a powwow with some of the hands. We're at the bend where the Little Arkansas feeds into the Arkansas and we can't cross."

"How come?" Becker asked.

"Bunch of farmers are askin' us to pay a toll. Two bits a head. It'll be four bits by tomorrow. They got us outnumbered and outgunned."

"That's a hell of a note. Mind if I ride on up to the campfire and grab some of that coffee? I know Miles Blaine slightly. Seen him a time or two with his pa and up at the Lazy J some time back."

"Sure. I'm just ridin' nighthawk with another man on the other end. You'll find a bunch yonder at the fire."

"I'm so damned tired, I hope I can make it that far."

"Good luck," Curly Bob said, and continued his slow ride around the herd, the tune back to humming on his lips.

Becker rode to the campfire, Jock staggering and zigzagging as they rounded the bedded-down herd. He dropped off his horse and started to crumple when Al Corning grabbed him.

"Where did you come from?" Tad said as Al set Becker down on a clump of grass near the fire.

"I know where he came from," Miles said. "He rides for my brother, Jared. Will Becker, ain't it?"

Will nodded desultorily.

"You want some coffee?" Al asked.

"Yeah, that might help," Becker said. "Hello, Tad. Long time no see."

"Heard you was in Leavenworth," Tad said. "Your sister?"

"Yeah, I got back a while ago. My sister's doin' okay, I reckon."

Miles passed a cup of coffee to Becker. "How come you're not with Jared?" he asked.

Becker blew on his steaming coffee and took a sip. The liquid burned his tongue. "Jared sent me on ahead to scout you out," Becker said.

"How far back is he?" Miles asked.

"He's runnin' the herd day and night. I'd say less'n twenty miles by mornin'. Maybe catch up to you by tomorrow evenin'."

"Well, that might help solve our problem," Tad said.

Miles shot Tad a look of incredulity. "Jared wouldn't piss on me if I was on fire," Miles said.

"Well, he can't cross the river neither without payin' the toll to that Pete Boggs," Tad said.

"Pete Boggs?" Becker said.

"That's the name of the man who's leadin' all them sodbusters at the crossing," Tad said. "A stubborn, mule-headed son of a bitch."

"Yeah, I know the man," Becker said. "He rode with Quantrill durin' the war. He's a dangerous bastard. I run into him a time or two, most recently when I was headin' back from Leavenworth. He's got a thirst for blood."

"And money," Miles said.

"Yeah, that too," Becker said as he raised the cup to his lips once again.

"We were just deciding what to do in the morning," Miles said. "I think we ought to drive the herd way around Boggs and find another crossing."

"I think we'd have Boggs right on top of us like ugly on a ape," Tad said.

"You likely would, Tad," Becker said. "He's been takin' tolls from every Texan who drives a herd into Kansas. And he's got some renegade Kiowa on his side if he needs 'em."

"What?" Miles said. "Injuns?"

"Yep, Injuns. Kiowa that don't recognize treaties. Savages that still take white scalps and hang 'em in their lodges."

"I ain't seen nary an Injun," Al said.

"All Boggs has to do is send up a smoke signal," Becker said, "and them Kiowa will be down on you like a herd of wild buffalo."

The men around the fire sat silent for several moments as Becker continued to sip his coffee. Miles noticed that his eyes were droopy, and that his horse had lain down and closed its own eyes.

Finally, Tad spoke up. He took a puff off his cigarette and blew a perfect ring that floated over the fire like a ghostly doughnut. He watched it fall apart in the faint breeze wafting off the river.

"I got an idea," he said. "Might work."

"Let's hear it," Miles said, without much enthusiasm.

"You ain't gonna like it, more'n I do," Tad said. "But it's the onliest way we're goin' to ford that river without paying blood money to Boggs."

The men all looked at Tad. Miles nodded for him to go ahead and divulge his idea.

"Let's say we get the herd up and movin' before it's light out," Tad said. "We run 'em up to the river all in a bunch, wide as we can get 'em, then push 'em into the fordin' place and fire off our guns all at once. One of us could take a long rifle and pick out Boggs and put his damned lamp out. My bet is the rest of them sodbusters would panic and run off like a bunch of scared rabbits. What do you think, Miles?"

Miles shook his head. He picked up a stick of kindling and began to draw lines in the dirt between his boots.

"I don't know," he said. "If it's plumb dark, how would you pick out Boggs from the rest of them farmers? And what if the others don't run, but start shootin' our cattle while they're swimmin' in the water?"

There was a moment of silence.

"They won't run," Becker said. "None of 'em. They all fought with Quantrill's Raiders and they're all as bloodthirsty as Boggs."

"You know 'em?" Al asked.

Becker looked sheepish and hung his head. "I rode with Quantrill myself. I was born in Topeka."

"Shit fire," Al said.

"And save the matches," Pedro Coronado cracked. He had been silent the entire time, but now he was animated and wore a big grin on his face.

"Them boys won't only shoot the cattle like ducks in a rain barrel," Becker said, "but they'll shoot you too. And they're all crack shots. With either rifle or pistol. When I was with 'em, we had cap n' ball and them boys never missed when we was raidin' over in Missouri."

"It's a good idea, Tad," Miles said. "But I can't risk all our lives and we'd probably lose a lot of the herd."

"It's the only way I can see us crossing that river without payin' a toll," Tad said.

"If you had a big enough herd now," Coronado piped in. "And a few more men."

"Eh?" Miles said as he swung his gaze onto Pedro. "What are you getting at?"

"Becker said that your brother, Jared, might get here sometime this day or by sunset. Then we would have a bigger herd and more men to fight the farmers."

"He's got a point," Tad said.

"A good point, maybe," Miles agreed.

He stopped his scratches with the stick of kindling and gazed into the fire.

What would Jared say to such a plan? Would he even consider siding with him to fight off Boggs and his men? Jared had never forgiven him for marrying Caroline and now there was no telling what he would say when he heard the bad news. He would probably blame him for Caroline's tragedy since it had been one of his hands who had beaten her half to death. Moreover, he had taken Earl Rawson away from Jared in the first place.

It was not a good situation, he knew. But he also knew that they had to cross the river and get both herds to Salina sometime before June first, and the month of May was slipping away like quicksilver on a hot skillet.

He watched as the cup fell from Becker's

hand. He toppled over and hit the ground, fast asleep.

It was curious, Miles thought, how fate had stepped in, not only with Leeds catching up to him with the bad news about Caroline, and Becker with the news that Jared was hot on his heels, but with all those armed men waiting across the river. Not only was fate a part of his life now, but what he did that day and the next might well decide his destiny.

CHAPTER 27

Jared set the pace as his herd forged forward. He and Paco also set the course, allowing the cattle to swing wide of the river so that it was no longer traveling over chewed and trampled grasses, but wading through belly-high fodder that was as fresh as the Kansas air itself.

"At least we know we're on the right track," Jared said to Paco.

"Pretty big herd passed this way, Jared. Bigger than ours."

"Which means Miles stands to make more money than me."

Paco said nothing. He knew that Miles and Jared were at odds with each other. Over a woman. He had met Caroline once and had developed an instant dislike of her. There was something in the way she looked at him when they met that made him think she would be an unfaithful wife. He had been relieved when she married Miles instead of Jared, but he kept his thoughts to himself. He dreaded to think that Caroline would be on the Lazy J. She was trouble and everybody but Jared could see it.

The herd trotted after them, snatching tufts of grass when they could, always trying to veer toward the river. But the hands kept them on the straight and narrow, yelling at the slow ones, waving their hats at the ones who wanted to bolt or stray. It was a brutal pace, but they were eating up the miles.

Paco stayed behind Jared with an eye on the leaders, ready to turn them back if they turned toward the river. A flanker on the right had little to do but urge the cattle on as if he were running them into a chute at the stockyards.

Toward evening, the herd veered closer to the river, and Paco sensed a change in the air. He could hear the mallards and pintails chuckling in the river and he saw flights of ducks heading for the distant cornfields to feed. Doves whistled past every so often and hawks floated over the fields on the other side of the Arkansas.

"Rider up ahead," Jared called over his shoulder. "And I see cattle grazin' all over the place."

"Must be the Rocking M," Paco said.

"They're not movin', that's for sure."

Paco took off his hat and waved to the lone rider patrolling the tail end of the herd ahead of them. The rider waved back and rode out to meet them.

"Howdy," Jared said. "What outfit you with?"

"I ride for the Rocking M," Joadie Lee said. "Ain't you Jared Blaine?"

"Yeah, I am. You know where Miles is?"

"Him and Tad Rankin are up at the river bend, I reckon. We been stuck here for two days."

"Stuck here?"

"Yes, sir. They's a bunch of dirt farmers won't let us cross less'n we pay 'em a toll. Yesterday it was two bits and now they want four bits, the bastards."

Paco and Jared exchanged looks.

"Paco, you hold the herd here," Jared said. "I'll ride up and see what's going on."

"*Ten cuidado,* Jared," Paco said in Spanish. "Be careful."

Paco turned around and stopped the herd from moving forward. He waved to one of the flankers.

"Let the cattle go to water," he yelled.

Chet Loomis waved back and passed the word along to the other drovers. The cattle began to walk toward the riverbank and

Paco let out a long breath. Ducks fluttered up from the water as the cows intruded on them and began to drink. Mallards, teal, redheads, and canvasbacks rose and flew off to the west where there were corn and wheat fields stretching to the horizon.

"Uh-oh," Tad said when he saw the lone rider trotting up to them. "I'd recognize the cream-colored gelding anywheres."

Miles turned around and saw his brother. "Yep, that's Jared and Puddin'," he said.

"This should be interesting," Tad said.

"You hold your tongue, Rankin," Miles snapped, and Tad realized right off that the meeting between the two brothers was liable not to go well.

"Who's that?" asked Boggs, who had been talking to Tad and Miles.

"That's my brother," Miles said.

"Well, well, well," Boggs said. He rubbed his palms together and flashed a gleeful smile. "More Texas cattle, I reckon."

"Look, Mr. Boggs," Miles said, "I asked you real polite if you'd let us pay ten cents a head on credit. Let us cross and we'll pay you when we come back this same way."

"No deal, Blaine. It's four bits a head, and if you wait another day, it'll cost you six bits a head."

"That's robbery," Miles said.

"I own the river, Mr. Blaine. Any outfit that crosses has got to pay for the privilege. No exceptions."

Jared rode up and dismounted. "Miles," he said, then looked at Tad. "Tad Rankin. So Pa sent you to nursemaid my brother."

"There's no need to be sarcastic, Jared," Miles said. "But I want you to meet Mr. Peter Boggs here. He says he owns the river and he's trying to extort money from me I don't have."

"Mr. Blaine," Boggs said, extending his scarred and wrinkled hand, a hand burned by the sun and cracked from too many early-morning milkings.

Jared looked down at Boggs and didn't offer his hand.

"You don't own this or any other river, far as I'm concerned," Jared said. "And we won't pay you one damned cent to cross it."

"Take a look across the river, Blaine," Boggs said, the false smile gone from his face. "You see those men. They say you pay me two bits a head for every cow in your herd that crosses this bend."

"Is that a threat?" Jared asked.

"You can call it a promise. Them boys are itchin' to crack them rifles and they'll drop men as well as cows if you try and run your

251

herd acrost without payin'."

Jared turned to Miles. "What did you tell Boggs here?"

Miles told him of his most recent offer.

"Ten cents a head on credit," he said.

"I ain't payin' this sodbuster one red cent," Jared said.

He stepped up to Boggs and bent his head so that his face was only inches away.

"You get on back across, Boggs. We'll rest the herd tonight and come mornin' we're crossing this river. Far as I'm concerned, it's still a free country, even here in Kansas."

"You got it right, Blaine," Boggs retorted. "It's a free country, except right here at this bend in the river. If you bring your herd across now, it's two bits a head. You wait until morning it's fifty cents."

"Get your ass out of here, Blaine, before I break your chiselin' neck."

Jared's hand dropped to the butt of his pistol, and the move was not lost on Pete Boggs. He backed away, throwing his hands up in the air in mock surrender.

"You're sure as hell gonna have blood on your hands if you stick one damned cow in that river without payin'," Boggs said as he walked back down to the ferry raft where some of his men were waiting, out of ear-shot.

"Well, Jared," Miles said, "I guess you told him."

"He might as well pull his bandanna up over his ugly face," Jared said. "He's a damned bandit."

He turned around and saw Will Becker standing next to him. He had walked up without Jared hearing him.

"Howdy, boss," Becker said. "You made good time with the herd."

"And you didn't come back and report that Miles was stuck here."

"He was plumb tuckered last night," Tad said. "Fell asleep while drinkin' his coffee."

"Well, you ain't ridin' for the Rockin' M, Will."

"Nope, but I heard what you said to Pete Boggs. Put a little scare in me, to tell you the truth."

"You scared of Boggs?"

"It ain't just him, Jared. Look at those men over on the other side of the river. I knowed 'em all, rode with them in the war. Course we was all just kids then, but they were a bloodthirsty bunch. I seen 'em kill women and children without battin' an eye, murdered them with cap n' ball .44s just like they was shootin' rats in a henhouse."

Jared looked across the river. He looked at each man.

"Well, they ain't kids no more," he said.

"Jared, Will here says they can call in renegade Kiowas to fight with 'em."

"That so?" Jared looked at Will again.

Will nodded.

"Then we better get ready for war," he said, " 'cause I'm crossin' that blamed river in the morning."

Jared looked at Miles. His gaze was steady and Miles knew he wanted him to agree with him.

"I think you and I better have a talk, Jared," Miles said. "You have the same idea that Tad had last night. I thought he was wrong and that we'd lose a lot of cattle and most of our men. We're outnumbered and outgunned, pure and simple. But if you and I join forces and run our herds together, Tad's plan might work."

"I'd like to hear about it," Tad said, kicking a dirt clod with the heel of his boot. "Your cookie got any hot coffee we can guzzle down?"

"He sure does," Will said, then flashed a sheepish grin at Jared. "I just had me a cup."

"You get on back and tell Paco to ride up to the Rockin' M chuck wagon. We'll put our heads together and see if we can run this Boggs clear out of Kansas."

Becker turned and walked to his horse,

which was ~~ground~~-tied to a nearby bush. He mounted up and rode off toward the Lazy J herd.

"Let's get that coffee, Miles," Jared said, "and talk this whole thing over."

They could see the chuck wagon from where they stood. Smoke rose from a fire burning in a ring a few yards from it. As they walked closer, they could smell the boiling coffee.

The setting sun smeared the sky with red, gold, and silver, painted the cloud faces a royal purple, and seamed their linings with radiant silver. Ducks flew over the two rivers, quacking as their wings beat the air. There was a tang in the air, an aroma of river water, cattle, horses, and sweat-laden men that nearly smothered the aroma of the Arbuckles' coffee.

Miles wondered how he was going to tell Jared about Caroline and whether or not this was the right time to even mention it. He was glad that they were walking together and that they would talk. He had missed his brother, but knew that Jared had never forgiven him for taking Caroline away from him and marrying her.

He vowed, as they approached the chuck wagon, that he would only mention Caroline if Jared brought her up, asked about her.

And, deep inside, he hoped Jared never would, at least until the drive was over and they were celebrating in a Salina saloon.

CHAPTER 28

Pete Boggs stepped ashore on the other side of the river. The men waiting there saw that he was fuming with anger.

"What's up, Pete?" one of the men asked.

Pete looked at Ralph Taggert, who had asked the question.

"We got a real firecracker on our hands, boys," Boggs said to the group. "Blaine's brother, name of Jared, has got him a herd and aims to cross without payin' the toll."

"To hell with him," another man spoke up. His name was Dave Elkins, a bearded thirty-year-old farmer with a twice-broken nose and scars on his face from scalp to chin. He puffed on a corncob pipe and had a bottle of corn liquor tucked in his back pocket.

"That one, Jared Blaine, he don't back down none. I don't know how many men he has with him, but with two herds and a passel of drovers, we might have a fight on our hands."

"Didn't I see Will Becker over yonder?" Ralph said. "Sure looked like him. All growed up now."

"Yeah, like the rest of us," Boggs said. "Yeah, I saw Will walkin' up behind the Blaines before I left. The son of a bitch is a Texan now, I reckon."

"Maybe he ain't," a man named Hardy Coolidge said, a rawboned pig farmer with scars of acne pocking his wizened face. Like the others, he wore overalls and work boots with large heels. He smelled of swine and a dozen other barnyard aromas.

"Will never was one of us," Ralph said. "Even when we rode with Quantrill. He had no stomach for fightin'."

"You're wrong there, Ralph," Boggs said. "He done his share of killin' when we was chased by Federals out of Springfield."

"Yeah," Hardy said. "He was a pretty good shot, I recollect."

"Well, we got our hands full, that's for sure," Boggs said. "We got to stay on guard all night and wait to see what happens to-morry."

"We're low on terbaccy," one of the men said. "And ain't enough coffee left to scald a cat."

"One or two of you hightail it into town

and fetch us some terbaccy and coffee 'fore it gets dark," Boggs said. "Ralph, you get the fire started and we'll gnaw on pork ribs this evenin'."

The men scattered to perform various tasks. Boggs took Hardy aside and spoke to him as he looked across the river.

"Hardy, you and Dave take the first watch. Keep an eye on that raft and make sure none of them cowboys crosses the river tonight. I'll get two of the boys to spell round midnight. Can you do this for me?"

"Sure, Pete. I done guard duty plenty when we was with Quantrill. Only we was called 'pickets' then."

Boggs smiled and slapped Hardy on the back.

"Good man, Hardy," he said.

Boggs told Dave the same thing and then, after looking at the cook fire across the river, said: "You know what I forgot to tell them Blaine boys?"

"Nope," Dave said.

Boggs chuckled.

"I forgot to tell 'em that we charge ten dollars extry for wagons, chuck or otherwise."

Dave, a rather dull fellow, did not grasp the humor of Boggs's statement. "Why, we sure better tell 'em next time you talk to 'em, Pete."

"I sure will, Dave," Boggs said, and walked over to where some of the men were unwrapping knapsacks filled with kindling wood and dry branches retrieved from the river over the past few days.

"I need two men to stand guard from midnight till dawn," he said. "Dave and Hardy are takin' the first shift."

Two men spoke up and raised their hands. Another was unwrapping a bundle of cured pork ribs and laying out the cooking irons.

"I hope them boys get back from town afore it closes up," Jesse Coombs said as he set dried grass beneath wood shavings to start the fire. He looked off down toward the town of Great Bend, which was nearly two miles away.

"Simpkins will keep his store open long as someone's got coin to lay on his counter," Boggs said. He hated towns and commerce, merchants and drummers. If he had his way, people would still be using the barter system and there would be no greed such as existed in the settlements. He believed in men exchanging services for goods and that man was meant to live by the sweat of his brow.

That is why he hated the cattlemen who came up from Texas and took money out of Kansas.

"Greed begets greed," he always said. "And them what holds slaves are the greediest of all." He had been saying that since the war and believed it still. He was glad that the North had won, but he still knew of folks who held slaves and believed the Southerners, including Texans, still worked sharecropping whites and blacks in their cotton and tobacco fields.

Boggs was a man filled with anger, and as he prepared himself mentally for a fight the next day, he envisioned his men eating fresh beef for supper the following night, while dead Texans floated in the river like poleaxed hogs, their bodies swelling up in the sun until the buttons on their shirts popped.

"Them Texans will pay the toll," he told the other men at supper. "One way or another, they're gonna pay."

The men cheered his words as the fire shot bright golden sparks in the air and the smell of pork ribs floated across the river to the camp of the Texans.

The night sky filled with stars and the moon rose like a graceful swan, beaming down an almost majestic light on the Kansas prairie.

CHAPTER 29

Before dark, Jared and Paco rode along the Little Arkansas River to assess their chances of crossing at another ford. They rode as far as the little town of Great Bend, which was an assemblage of mud huts and clapboard shacks, a couple of places with false fronts. It appeared to be a poor town, with only a few inhabitants. They saw a hardware store and a dry goods establishment. He read a sign in one store window that read PURDY'S DRUGS & SUNDRIES, and another that looked like a warehouse bore the legend CANTWELL'S FARM EQUIPMENT. Simpson's General Store stood out as the largest and Jared figured it served the farmers for many miles around. In the distance they saw small hardscrabble farms and fields of ankle-high corn and small fields of alfalfa and clover.

"Can't cross anywhere near this town," Jared said. "We'd have cattle running into stores, and we'd get chased by women with rolling pins and shopkeepers with pitchforks and iron skillets."

"This is not a good place," Paco agreed.

They rode in the other direction, two miles above where the herds were being held. A man on horseback, with a rifle at present arms, followed them on the opposite side of the river.

"Water looks too deep up this way," Jared said.

"The river gets narrow. We would have to swim the cattle across. Some would get drowned, I think."

"No, the only place seems to be where that ferry raft is. It's wide and shallow there and that's the crossing marked on the map my pa gave me."

"Then that is where we must cross," Paco said, and there was no fear in his voice. But he, like Jared, knew they would have to fight their way through those Kansas jayhawks. There would be bloodshed on both sides.

The two men returned to camp and supper around the chuck wagon fire. Cookie served up red beans, beef, and fresh corn bread, along with boiled cabbage and peaches out of airtights. There was hot, rich coffee and lively conversation about everything but crossing the river the next day.

Then, when the meal was finished, Miles brought up the subject, addressing his brother, Jared.

"Well, brother, you and Paco there looked up and down the river. What do you think?"

"I think we must cross in the morning. At first light. If those jaspers on the other side stay up all night, they'll be off their feed and that gives us a slight advantage."

"Do you have a plan, Jared?"

The men at the campfire all leaned forward to hear what Jared had to say. In the momentary silence, they heard ducks chattering on the river and the far-off yap of a coyote. Bullbats soared like wraiths high above the fire, darting and weaving through the sable night, faded silver coins on their wings.

"The way I see it," Jared said, "we have a couple of choices. We can bring the entire herd, meanin' your cattle and mine, put them in the water, and see what Boggs and his men do."

"They'll likely start shooting the lead cattle," Tad said, a cigarette dangling from his mouth, smoke scratching his eyes like shaved onions, which made them water and blink.

"Yeah, that's a prime possibility," Jared said.

"We could lose a lot of cattle with twenty men firin' repeatin' rifles," Al Corning piped in.

"Or," Jared said, "we can strike them first."

"You mean just start shooting across the river?" Miles said.

Jared looked over at Becker, who was on his second cup of coffee. "Will, you fought in the war. What do you think? Or have you thought about it?"

"We really didn't ever run acrost a situation like this when I was with Quantrill," Becker said. "But I knowed some tactics from just listenin' to the officers talk at night."

"And was there something said about fighting across a river?" Jared asked.

"Not exactly, but some of the officers mentioned digging trenches during a siege. They called them 'parallels' and said an army could keep digging those parallels in circles around a town or a fort and pretty soon the troops would be at the gate and they could bring a cannon up and breach the fortifications."

"Hmmph," Jared uttered. "There ain't no town, nor no fort. There's just that blamed river, wide as a cow pasture."

"We could dig trenches," Tad said. "For cover."

"We maybe got four shovels between us," Roy said. "We'd have to dig all night and then maybe . . ."

"I thought we could use the chuck wagon for some cover," Norm Collins said. "Put men on their bellies underneath, some in the bed, and others behind, in front and back."

"All good suggestions," Jared said. "We could run the chuck wagon up close to the bank and parallel. Put some of our rifles behind that."

"Sounds good to me," Miles said.

Jared looked around at the men sitting at the fire. He mentally counted how many hands he had, and those who were riding as nighthawks around the herd.

He looked again at Becker. "What would you do, Will?"

The attentions of all the men shifted to Becker, who set his coffee cup down between his boots and looked at Jared with piercing eyes.

"I don't like the idea of bein' in a trench, to tell you the truth. Or hidin' behind that chuck wagon. We're all horsemen. We live on our horses. We work on them. We can make our horses run or walk or jump over fences. When I fought with Quantrill, I was cavalry. We marched and we fought on horseback."

"Good point," Jared said. "And all pretty good suggestions."

"Are you going to run this show, Jared?" Miles asked, his voice soft and nonthreatening. He asked it of a brother he had grown up with, a brother he loved dearly and whom he respected, despite their differences over Caroline.

"Somebody's got to call the shots," Jared said. "You have any preferences, Miles?"

Miles thought there might have been a tinge of sarcasm in Jared's tone, but he couldn't be sure. But he felt the old hostilities rising between them. And, with what they had to face on the morrow, he didn't want to quarrel with Jared or rub him the wrong way.

"The way I see it," Miles said, "this cow camp ain't exactly a democracy. Yet we all are facing the same decision, the same danger. We got to have a leader, but we all got to have a say in who that leader is and back him all the way. If you want the job, it's yours. And if you don't, you can appoint your foreman or anyone you trust to lead us through this dark valley."

"Miles, you got a poet hiding somewhere

inside you," Jared said. "But I agree. We got to all come to terms on how we're goin' to make this crossing tomorrow. And there's sure as hell goin' to be lead flyin', in both directions."

"So, boss," Paco said, "how are we to do this? The sodbusters have more men and I hear they are all good shots. I will fight and I think every man here will fight. But do we ride across with our guns and start shooting, or do we wait for them to shoot first?"

"Paco, you've got brains, I'll give you that," Jared said.

"Answer his questions, Jared," Miles prodded. "I want to know too. How do we get across that river with all of our cattle and the least number of injuries or deaths?"

Jared stood up. He walked around in a tight circle as if he were mulling over a plan of attack. He looked across the river at the glowing campfire and the silhouettes of the two men on guard. Then he returned to his place in the circle and sat down.

"Boggs is expecting us to fight," he said. "He knows we can't, or we won't, pay him his damned toll. But he's determined to keep us from crossing if he has to kill every one of us. Pa once told me, and he probably told Miles too, that when you got a big problem, it's like a big old bull is charging you, with its head down and hoofs a-flying. He said you can't run and you can't hide. He said you got to take the bull by the horns."

"Bulldog the son of a bitch," Curly Bob said. "Throw him to the ground."

"Exactly," Jared said.

"So how do we take this particular bull by the horns?" Miles asked, genuinely curious.

"All right," Jared said. "I've listened to all these suggestions. I've scouted the river with my foreman, Paco. I know some of you and heard tell of some of you. We are horsemen. We are cattlemen too. So we use what we have to fight those bastards over there."

Miles leaned forward, eager to hear what Jared had to say. The others held their breaths and looked thoughtful.

"No trenches," Jared said. "We'll use the chuck wagon for cover, but we'll have riders behind it, sittin' tall in the saddle, shootin' rifles. We're going to run the herd across that river. Yeah, we may lose a few head, but we're going to be drivin' and shootin'."

"That's what I wanted to hear," Tad said when Jared paused for a few seconds. "Bull by the horns."

"You're damned right," Al said. "Drive the cattle and shoot the soddies."

"Some men will have to ride the flanks,

keep the cattle streaming across. Some will just shoot from behind the wagon. Others will come ridin' up with more of the herd and keep their rifles hot. If you run out of rifle bullets, use your pistols. Ride, ride, ride, and shoot, shoot, shoot."

"Someone will have to time this all out," Roy said. "Make sure we hit the water in waves and keep the rifles firing as we cross."

"Miles, you can do that," Jared said. "You can watch and see who's still shooting and send men to take the places of those who fall."

Miles sucked in a breath. He started to shake his head, but he could see what his brother was driving at. They would cross the river in waves, riders on both sides of the herd, and keep them all moving so that they would have a mass of cattle and men pushing across, firing their weapons, and dodging bullets. It was bold, it was daring, and it could work, if they all pulled together. And if they all were directed by one man who could see all that was happening and know when to send other men into the fray.

"What about you, Jared?" Miles asked. "Where will you be?"

Jared looked at all the other men who were waiting to hear his answer. He knew men and he knew himself. He licked his lips and spoke to all of them while looking directly at his brother.

"I'm going to be in the lead," Jared said. "I'll take the leaders across and I'll be aimin' for that clod-kickin' little bastard, Pete Boggs, while me and Puddin' wade that river."

Some of the men smiled. Others looked sheepish and ashamed. There was not a man jack among them that didn't know that Jared had picked out for himself the most dangerous job of all.

They looked at him with admiration and respect.

Miles looked at Jared with a sense of dark foreboding. He wanted to say something, but he would not dash the men's hopes.

They had a leader. They had a man they could follow through death's door.

Yes, he was filled with dread, but he also looked at his brother with a newfound respect.

"Let's get some sleep," Miles said, "those of us who can. Short watches and make sure you got plenty of ammunition, that your rifles are fully loaded and your pistols working. Good night, everybody."

Jared smiled and stood up. He walked over to Miles and looked down at him.

"See you in the morning, brother," he said.

"When you ride out tomorrow, Jared, you be careful, hear?"

Jared said nothing. He walked away and disappeared into the night with his horse, Paco alongside him, leading his own horse.

Miles stood up, looked at Cookie. "You put that wagon parallel to the water before morning, Cookie."

"I will. Good night, Miles."

The ducks on the river were silent and the bullbats were gone. There was only the stillness of the night and the distant winking of stars, the floating globe of the moon and the faint lapping of waters as two rivers sang their wise old songs that only a god could understand.

CHAPTER 30

It was still dark as an anthracite coal pit when Jared rode up to the chuck wagon the next morning. He was not riding his buckskin, Puddin', but the black horse he had borrowed from Paco. He dismounted and walked over to the small group of men gathered by the small fire. A coffeepot hung from the irons, burbling and spewing freshets of steam through its spout.

"Here's you some coffee, Jared," Cookie said, handing Jared a tin cup he had just poured half-full. "Watch your lips and tongue."

"Good advice, Cookie," Jared said, and there was a joviality about him that surprised Miles, who was sipping coffee from his own cup.

"It's still pretty dark, Jared," Miles said. "But we're ready when you are."

"Soon as I finish my coffee, we'll start running the herd across the river. My men and yours are ready to go when I give the word."

"I'm nervous," Miles said, and held out a shaking hand to show his brother.

"The nerves will go away as soon as you hear the first crack of a rifle from across the river."

"That's not very reassuring, Jared."

"Think about the work to be done and keep your head down, brother," Jared said.

Miles gave out a tremulous chuckle and steadied his shaking hand.

Jared surveyed the dark river. He had been mulling over his plan since after midnight when the guards changed shifts. Now he had made his decision and began to issue orders to his and Miles's men.

"I want to leave this space open," Jared said, pointing to the landing where the ferry docked. "I want the herd spread out, a mile on each side, and at my signal, you put the cattle into the water and drive them across."

Paco and Roy listened intently and nodded. So too did Tad, Al, and Miles.

"Where will you cross?" Miles asked.

Jared raised his left hand and sliced the air as if he were wielding a meat cleaver. "I'm going straight across, with cattle on either side of me. As soon as I see a target, I'll start shooting."

"That sounds pretty shaky to me, Jared," Miles said.

"The main thing is to keep the cattle moving across the river. When the guns go off, I don't want cattle stampeding all over the place. Miles, you keep that herd moving. Use as many men as you need to push, push, push."

"Will do," Miles said. He set his empty coffee cup on the ground next to a wagon wheel and began to give orders to the men at the head of the herd. He sent Curly Bob to the rear of the Lazy J herd to tell the drag riders to push the herd toward the river. "And don't stop for anything. Keep your eyes peeled for strays and run every head across that river."

Curly Bob galloped off to spread the word.

Jared rode down to the bank of the river and looked across.

It was still dark, but he could see the shadowy silhouettes of the men across the river. They had a small fire, but it was partially shielded by stones piled to block off the light.

He was ready.

Jared drew in a breath and raised his hand high above his head. He let out his breath and dropped his hand. He prodded Paco's horse with his blunt spurs and entered the flowing water of the river. He hunched over the saddle horn so that he presented no silhouette.

He heard the splashing and saw cattle entering the river on his right and on his left. He smiled with satisfaction. Mentally, he counted off the yards to the other bank. More than a hundred.

But the water was not as swift where he had entered. It was wide and shallow at that place. Some of the cattle at both ends would have to swim some, but they ought to make it if they didn't panic and tire themselves out by flailing the water with their hooves.

He heard some of the cowhands yell at the cattle and he waited until more white-faces were in the river. Some swam toward him and he spurred the horse to move ahead.

From across the river, Jared heard a man shout the alarm.

"Here they come."

Men cursed and Jared saw some scramble for their rifles. Others grabbed at saddled horses.

Then he heard the whip-crack of a rifle and saw a plume of blue and orange flame partially illuminate a man's face, a man who held the rifle and was aiming low, at the cattle.

From behind him, rifles crackled as cow-hands began to shoot from behind the chuck wagon. The air sizzled with the buzz of lead bullets and some whistled past his ears. He heard splashes. A cow reared its head and fell over with a resounding splash. Men shouted from both sides of the river, cursing and warning, firing their rifles in rapid succession.

Jared kept low and kept his horse moving forward toward the opposite bank. He heard bullets splash around him. He looked at the flashes from the rifle muzzles and tried to pick out a target. He wanted Boggs, but he would take down any man he could line up in his sights.

He slipped his rifle from its boot and levered a cartridge into the firing chamber. He hugged the horse's neck and extended the rifle along its left side. The barrel moved from side to side and up and down. He could not get a clear shot.

One man walked down to the bank and Jared sat up slightly and put the rifle to his shoulder. He lined up the front blade with the rear buckhorn and saw the man's chest in a direct line of sight.

Jared held his breath and squeezed the trigger.

His rifle exploded, the recoil ramming the

stock against his shoulder. Flame and lead spurted from the muzzle and he heard the whoosh of air as the bullet sped toward its target.

The man screamed and grabbed at his chest. His rifle slipped from his hands and tumbled down off the bank and into the water. Then the man toppled forward and hit the water with a splash. A man up on the bank cursed and fired at Jared, who turned his horse and then turned it again to avoid being hit.

A bullet whizzed close to Jared's ear and he felt the hackles rise on the back of his neck. He sat up then and swung his rifle, looking for another target, higher up on the bank.

More rifles boomed and more bullets ripped through the water around him.

From behind, he could hear the cowhands shooting and he saw one of the farmers stagger and fall to his knees.

Cattle swarmed around him, in a panic. They were wading through water up to their chests, pushing against the current, floundering to keep their footing. Their white faces were turned upward and he could see the pink of their noses as they continued to the other bank, pushed by the cattle behind them and the men yelling them on as if they were all in a footrace at a county fair.

Jared could no longer find a target. Instead, he just aimed and guessed, pulled the trigger. He levered cartridge after cartridge into the receiver of the Winchester until the magazine was empty. He shoved the rifle back in its boot and drew his Colt six-gun. There was no time to reload the rifle.

He saw that he wasn't even halfway across and the bullets came fast and furious. He tried to wade the horse in a zigzag, but the water was too swift and the horse was tiring too fast.

In the east there was a small rent in the sky and light spilled through the fissure like cream rising in a churn. Shadowy men on the other side were lying down and picking their targets, while others rode horses up and down the high bank. These were shooting at cattle and trying to unseat horsemen who had entered the river and were driving the cattle.

It made Jared sick to see cattle go under, leaving a bloody froth to be washed downstream before they reemerged, belly up, their hooves stiffening in the throes of death as they tumbled in the current.

He passed the midway point of the river, and now that there was some light, he saw the men who were shooting at him. He cocked his pistol and swung it toward a man who was using the raft for cover. He squeezed the trigger and the pistol bucked in his hand. He saw the man duck as the bullet whined just over his head. Then the man put his rifle to his shoulder and began to shoot at Jared.

He recognized the man as the light in the east grew stronger.

It was Pete Boggs, and he used a post for cover.

Jared fired again, but his horse jerked in the current just then and he knew his shot had gone wild.

Boggs took aim and fired.

Jared felt a sharp pain in his left shoulder. Seconds later, his arm went numb and he felt the hot trickle of blood running down his arm on the inside of his tattered sleeve. He gulped in air and grabbed the saddle horn with his left hand. The hand seemed to have no feeling in it and slipped off the saddle horn to dangle uselessly at his side.

He fired his pistol again at Boggs, squinting to block out the pain that was now shooting down his arm and across his chest.

Jared turned his horse. He headed straight for Boggs. His stomach churned with a sudden sickness and he felt the bile roil up in his throat. He slumped down over the saddle horn, felt it press against his flaming chest. The horn seemed to take away some of the pain.

His horse waded forward, struggling with each step. Jared dug his spurs deep into the horse's flanks as he stared ahead, his eyes filling with tears, Boggs just a blur, the barrel of his rifle spitting out sparks and lead.

He heard the smack of a bullet, and the horse quivered from the blow. Jared looked back and saw a furrow in the horse's rump. Blood oozed from the wound and the horse twisted beneath him, a woeful whinny of pain issuing from its throat.

Boggs turned to men up on the bank and yelled something at them. Jared couldn't understand what he was saying, but he heard the word "smoke" and saw men get up and run toward the small fire behind the stacked stones.

The horse struggled against the tug of the river's current, but drew closer to the landing on the other side.

The sun began to edge up over the horizon, its red rim like the top of a savage eye. Shadows stretched across the water and the prairie, the canvas on the chuck wagon lit up like a white sheet, and men's faces began to take on shape and features as if they were actors on a stage suddenly lit by footlights.

Jared watched as Boggs dropped to his knees and braced his rifle against the post where the lines from the raft tugged against the rocking waters of the river.

Jared drew in a breath and forced himself to aim the pistol. He steadied it against the horse's neck, lined up the sights, and held his breath. He squeezed the trigger. The explosion lifted the pistol in his hand, but he knew he had shot true.

He saw Boggs twitch as the bullet smacked into his breastbone. A crimson flower blossomed on Boggs's chest and he threw up his arms. The rifle floated above him for a split second, then crashed onto the raft.

Boggs tumbled backward, mortally wounded.

Men on the bank turned to see Boggs go down, then swung their rifles to take aim at Jared, who, once again, slumped over the pommel, his stomach retching as if he had swallowed arsenic poisoning.

Three rifles cracked from atop the bank.

Jared felt the slugs tear into his leg, his right arm, and across his chest. He felt as if a hot poker, cherry red, had burned into his sternum and he felt a black cloud descend over him.

Fire seemed to burn in every pore. He holstered his pistol and grabbed the saddle horn with both hands, despite the searing pain that seemed to strike him from every direction.

He hung on for dear life, but the blackness took away his sight and blotted out his mind.

And, somewhere, in a brief glimmer of light in that terrible darkness, he encountered the scrap of a thought that told him he was going to die.

CHAPTER 31

Miles tried to make sense of it all through the din of bellowing cattle, shouting men, and rapid gunfire streaming from both sides of the river. He had never seen so many cattle in the water before. The men drove them off the bank in large numbers and never let up, yelling, waving their hats, and cursing the slow and hesitant ones.

He fired his own rifle at shadows across the river. He never knew if he hit anyone, but he shot at heads poking up, and men on horseback. He watched as cattle took bullets and rolled into the river with bullets through their heads. It made him sick to see the senseless slaughter.

He thought he saw one of his own, or Jared's, men go down. He could not be sure. He could not be sure of anything in the melee around him. He caught glimpses of Jared, who seemed to be almost motionless in the middle of the river. But when he looked again, he saw that his brother was making slow progress and was miraculously still alive and firing his rifle.

More and more cattle rushed up on both sides of the chuck wagon. Men, men he only barely recognized, drove them into the river and then rode back to drive more in behind them.

Cookie climbed out of the chuck wagon and ran off into the darkness when bullets ripped holes in the canvas top. As soon as he was out of range, he had to scramble to avoid being trampled by the surging herd of cattle. He ran to the river, where he flattened himself against a large rock that jutted from a small mound in a copse of young cottonwoods. A pair of mud hens jumped up from the river and flew south a few hundred yards before skidding to a stop in the middle of the Arkansas.

Ducks, startled by the noise of the herd and the gunfire, crisscrossed the sky with whistling wings and angry quacks. Their white bellies shone ghostly against the night sky as they climbed out of danger and abandoned the river for the far fields where they had fed for most of the night.

As the eastern horizon began to pale, Miles saw Joadie Lee Bostwick, his horse in the water up to its knees, twist in the saddle as a bullet tore into his abdomen. He doubled over and yelled something, but Miles couldn't understand him. Then Joadie Lee turned his horse and clapped spurs into its flanks, headed back to the shore he had left moments before. He rode out of the water and then toppled from his horse.

Paco rushed to Joadie Lee's side and pried the rifle from his hands.

"Lie still," Paco said. "Where are you hit?"

"I dunno," Joadie Lee gasped. "My gut, I think."

Paco felt the sticky blood oozing from the drover's abdomen. When he pressed on the small hole, Joadie Lee lost consciousness. Paco turned him over and felt down the wounded man's back. There was an exit wound oozing blood on Joadie Lee's right side. He pulled the bandanna from around his neck and stuffed one end of it in the hole, then turned Joadie Lee over.

"Hold on, Joadie Lee," Paco said, but when he bent down and put his ear to the man's mouth, he knew that the cowhand was gone. He stood up and looked across the river at the stick figures of the men shooting their rifles. He raised his rifle to his shoulder, picked out a running man, waited until he stopped, then squeezed the trigger. The bullet from Paco's rifle hit the man in the side. He screamed, dropped his rifle, and ran several yards before he dropped.

The shooting went on, and Miles knew they would lose several head of cattle. He kept looking at his brother, and as the sun began to spray the prairie with its thin light, he saw Jared riding toward a man who looked like Pete Boggs.

Miles felt something grab at his heart. He saw Boggs turn and yell to the men up by the fire.

"Make the smoke," Boggs yelled, and the next minute, he saw Jared shoot the leader of the brigands. Then he saw men on the bank aim their rifles at Jared. He saw Jared jerk in the saddle. The horse twisted beneath him, and saw a puff of dust rise off the horse's flank. The horse crumpled and Jared slid into the water.

Miles saw men piling something on the fire until it bulged with gray smoke. Another man approached the smothered fire. He was carrying a horse blanket.

"Paco, Roy," Miles yelled. "Shoot that man trying to make a smoke signal. Everybody, drop that man."

Al and Roy began shooting. Miles dropped his rifle and ran to the river. He slipped off his boots and dived in. His hat floated off his head and floated into a clutch of cattle breasting their way through the water.

Paco shot the man with the blanket before he could drop it onto the fire. Another man crawled over and retrieved the blanket. He stood up to make smoke signals. Roy and Al both shot their rifles at the same time and the man fell face forward into the smoldering fire. He was stone dead and his body shut off oxygen, putting the fire out.

Miles swam to the place where he had seen Jared fall from his horse. It was light enough to see, and he reached out when he saw a leg and grabbed Jared's boot. He pulled himself close enough to wrap an arm around his brother's torso. He pulled him out of the water and turned him over. He grabbed Jared's head and turned his face to the sky.

Jared moaned and Miles breathed a sigh of relief.

"Jared," he said. "I got you. Just keep breathin', will you?"

Cattle swarmed around Miles and he batted the water with one hand to drive them away. He began to swim back to his side of the river, pulling Jared along with him. He flailed his legs, trying to find the bottom. His socks touched the bottom a few yards from shore and he waded to the bank, tugging Jared along under his arm. He climbed ashore and laid Jared down. Miles panted from the exertion. He was soaking wet, but he didn't care. He bent over his brother and listened for his breathing.

Paco and Al ran over. They were hunched down to lessen their value as targets. They fell to their knees beside Jared and Miles.

"Is he alive?" Paco asked.

"Yeah, but just barely. He's hurt bad," Miles said.

"Let's get him into the chuck wagon," Al said. "See if we can't bandage him up."

They knew that Cookie carried bandages, medications, salves, and liniments inside the wagon.

"Be careful," Miles said when Al took Jared by the legs and Paco lifted his upper body up. They took short steps and ran to the chuck wagon, Al pushing Jared as he would a wheelbarrow and Paco stepping backward. Miles ran alongside while bullets kicked up dirt clods all around them and tore furrows in the earth. They dodged cattle running toward the river until they reached the island where the chuck wagon was parked.

Miles scrambled into the back end and cleared a space for his brother, knocking aside bags of sugar and flour, tins of coffee and tobacco. There were blankets and pillows in the center where Cookie had slept during the night. He stuck his head out through the hole in the canvas.

"Give me his shoulders, Paco," Miles said, and reached for his brother with outstretched arms.

Al got underneath Jared's back and pushed upward. Paco climbed up and slid through the open end and helped Miles pull Jared inside the wagon. They laid him on the floorboards. Al climbed in behind them, his face drawn, his brows furrowed in worry.

"How is he?" Al asked.

"Let's get some pillows and blankets under him," Paco said.

He and Miles shoved every soft piece of dry goods they could find under Jared.

"I'll light a lantern," Al said.

"Be damned careful you don't set the canvas on fire," Paco warned.

Al struck a match and lifted the chimney of a lantern that had been hanging on one of the braces. Light filled the inside of the wagon.

Miles looked at his brother's face. Jared's eyes were closed and he had no color in his cheeks. Miles felt something squeeze his heart again and an emptiness crept into his stomach, a stomach fluttering with the dusty moth wings of fear.

"I–is he alive?" Miles whispered to Paco.

"He breathes," Paco said. "Hold that lantern up high, Al."

Paco began to run gentle fingers under Jared's shirt where it had been torn by a bullet. He felt blood and his fingers came away sticky with it. He saw the shoulder wound and found a bullet hole in Jared's leg. He felt around to the other side and touched another hole where the bullet had exited.

Paco sat back on his haunches.

"See what Cookie has in that medical box behind you, Miles. The one with the red cross on it."

Miles turned and saw the wooden box. He pulled it to him and set it between his legs. He lifted the latch and Al held the lantern over it so that all three men could look inside.

"There's bandages in there," Miles said, "and tins of salve and I don't know what all."

A head appeared at the rear of the wagon. It was Will Becker. "Need any help?" he asked.

"You know anything about gunshot wounds, Will?" Paco asked. "About medicines?"

"Some, I reckon. What you got?"

"Climb in here and take a look at this medicine box," Paco said.

Will stuck his rifle just inside the wagon, leaned it upright in one corner. He climbed in and looked first at Jared, then at the medicine kit in front of miles.

"I wish Doc was here," Miles murmured.

"Your pa?" Paco asked.

Miles nodded.

"Is he really a doctor?" Al asked.

"It's a long story," Miles said, then looked at Will, who was rummaging through the medical kit.

"Where's Jared hit?" he asked Paco.

"Three places, near as I can tell," Paco said. "He's got a hole in his right leg, a rip across his chest, and his shoulder looks like it was hit with a garden trowel. Don't know if any bones is broke."

"Let me see," Will said. He scooted around and looked first at Jared's shoulder.

"I seen wounds like this before. Bullet chewed up the meat, but missed the bone, I think."

He looked at the hole in Jared's legs.

"Give me that tin of Dr. Pettibone's All-Purpose Salve," he said to Miles. "Bullet went clean through. We can pack the hole plumb through and wrap a bandage around that leg."

"Can you do it?" Miles asked, his voice trembling with emotion.

"Sure, I plugged a few like this in the war. Mud and ground-up roots work just as well."

"What about the shoulder?" Paco asked.

"I can clean it with alcohol, then put this salve on it and wrap it real tight. Ought to work."

"What else?" Miles asked.

"It's that chest wound that bothers me most," Will said. "It don't look like much, but a bullet might have grazed his heart, or maybe scratched a lung. It's a funny-lookin' wound and hard to see if they's a bullet still in him or what."

Miles felt his heart plummet like a lead sash weight.

They heard cattle close by and some of them rubbed against the wagon. The wagon rocked and swayed on its wheels until the hands outside moved them back into line. Rifles continued to crackle and men yelled out warnings and threats. Sunlight streamed past the openings in the canvas and Miles could see cattle and drovers milling across the river.

"Did he take in any water when you dug him out of the river, Miles?" Will asked.

"I got to him pretty quick. But I don't know."

Will pushed on Jared's belly. Nothing came up his throat or gushed from his mouth.

"He seems all right," Al said.

Will finished bandaging Jared's shoulder. The wagon reeked of the foul-smelling salve.

"I don't know what to do about that chest wound," he said. "I'm kinda afraid to touch it much. We got to get Jared to a doctor. Quick as we can."

"I wonder if there's one in town," Miles said.

Will shook his head. "Ain't even a horse doctor in Great Bend."

"Damn," Miles said.

"I guess we can find one in Salina. Get someone to watch Jared and spoon him soup. He might make it."

"You think Jared's got a chance, Will?" Miles asked. His voice seemed far away, in someone else's body. He was choked up with emotion.

He didn't want Jared to die. No matter how bad things had been between them, he didn't want his brother to die out here on the prairie, far from home, far from Texas.

He closed his eyes and let the tears come. He felt a hand on his shoulder, but didn't

know who had touched him. He grabbed
Jared's hand in his and squeezed it. He
wanted to feel the life in it. He wanted to
feel the life in himself.

CHAPTER 32

The firing on both sides of the river seemed to be dying down when Paco and Al stepped down out of the chuck wagon.

Will and Miles stayed with Jared. Will went through the medicine box and got the bromides he needed for when Jared woke up.

"You need us, Miles, you just yell out," Paco said as he poked his head back inside the wagon. He grabbed his rifle from the corner where it still stood.

"What are you going to do, Paco?"

"I'm goin' to run cattle across and shoot every damned one of them sodbusters," he said.

Roy met Al and Paco when they walked back to their horses.

"How are we doing, Roy?" Paco asked.

"Them bastards are still tryin' to kill us and our cattle. But we took a passel of them out. I'm ready to ride acrost and finish the job. How about you?"

"How many head made the crossing, do you reckon?"

"Pert near two thousand, I figure. Just look at 'em all, will you?"

Paco and Al saw the cattle streaming past the farmers' camp, but there was no way to count them.

"So, another fifteen hundred head maybe," Paco said.

"Thereabouts," Roy said.

"Let's run some more across and keep goin' until we shoot every one of them sod-busters," Paco said.

Riders came to the river, drove cattle in, and once they were headed for the other side, rode back for more. Paco, Al, and Roy rode back to the herd and cut out twenty head and drove them into the river between the two herds already wading across. They headed straight for the landing.

Men across the river lay flat on the ground. They seemed to have plenty of ammunition and they were picking off cattle and shooting at cowhands with a vengeance.

"We'll use our pistols," Roy said. "We'll be close enough and they'll be easier to reload." They sheathed their rifles and plunged into the river behind the small bunch of cattle, hunkering over their saddles so as to present smaller targets.

The air sizzled with bullets traveling in both directions. When a bullet struck a rock, it caromed off in a keening whine. A bullet struck one of the whitefaces in the horn and made a dull thud. Blood gushed from the horn. The steer dipped its head and plowed on, bellowing its rage and pain.

Al picked targets and fired his double-action Colt at any head that popped up on the other side.

Roy saw a man trying to put more green wood on the fire, while another stood by with a horse blanket to make smoke.

"They keep tryin' to send a signal to the Kiowa we heard about," Al said.

Roy shot the man with the blanket, who twisted in a circle before he went down. The other man stopped putting wood on the fire and reached down for his rifle.

Paco shot him in the side. The man dropped to one knee and Paco shot him again from fifty yards away, his bullet ripping into the man's lower jaw and shooting it away.

"Pretty damned good shootin', Paco," Roy said.

"I practice a lot," Paco said. He spurred his horse and the animal splashed ashore behind the cattle and near the ferry raft. He slid to his left and hung tight to the saddle horn until Puddin' was on level ground. He was glad now that he had swapped horses with Jared, although his own had probably been shot or drowned when Jared was hit.

The sodbusters saw the riders coming up the bank and cattle heading their way, a phalanx of white-faced beasts.

One of them yelled, "Let's get the hell out of here, boys."

As Paco, Roy, and Al rode down on the remaining farmers, they turned to fire as they backed away from their camp and the river.

"Drop your weapons," Roy shouted to them.

But the farmers did not. Instead, they raised their rifles to their shoulders and took aim at the approaching cowhands.

That was a fatal mistake.

Roy, Al, and Paco shot almost simultaneously. The men screamed when they were hit. They fell and tried to shoot back. Those who ran away stopped and fired their rifles. Riders with the cattle cut them down as Paco, Roy, and Al dispatched the others, showing no mercy.

Finally, guns fell silent. Paco reloaded his pistol and his rifle.

"Is it over?" Roy asked.

"If no Injuns come ridin' up," Al said.

"Better reload, just in case," Paco said.

The three men joined the riders who were driving the herd away from the river. More cattle waded across at the ford and Paco rode back across to check on Jared and Miles. He found Cookie and told him to drive the chuck wagon across to the other side.

"Is the fightin' over?"

"Yep, but you got a hurt man in your wagon. I want you to head out for Salina after givin' us all grub for the trail."

"Who's hurt?"

"Jared Blaine," Paco said.

"Damn." Cookie brushed himself off and walked back to the chuck wagon. He looked inside and saw Jared lying there, flanked by Will and Miles. "I got to get grub for the trail. Then we'll head for Salina, get your brother to a doctor."

Miles just nodded. He was still too numb to speak. Jared was breathing hard and Will thought he might have swallowed some water when he fell into the river.

"If he gets the pneumony," Will said, "you know he breathed in some of that river water. But I'll tell you now, Miles, I saw the whole thing. You got to your brother just in time. You saved his life."

"If he lives," Miles said.

Cookie drove the wagon across the river without incident. He stopped beyond the herd that was still being rounded up by the hands and started piling beef jerky, hardtack, tins of beans and apricots on the sideboards.

Paco saw to it that all hands filled their saddlebags.

"You might all be eating rabbits before we get to Salina," he told them. "That chuck wagon is now an ambulance."

Cookie looked at the map Miles showed him.

"I can find my way," he said. "We'll make tracks."

"Thanks," Miles said. "Just don't bounce around too much."

Will said nothing. He was worried that a bullet, or a piece of lead, was still somewhere in Jared's chest. If so, the shrapnel could work its way to Jared's heart or shut down his lungs. He had seen men die long after being shot and judged to be cured by army surgeons. Jared was still unconscious and had begun to develop a fever. There wasn't enough heat on his forehead and face to worry about, but it was not a good sign.

Roy and Paco met after the entire herd had crossed the river.

"Looks like we got more trail bosses than ranch bosses, Paco," Roy said.

"I figure we got less than fifty miles to Salina. No use splitting up the herds."

"Nope. Be a waste of time. Cattle are all goin' to the same place, and what we've got is three brands."

"Doc said he would meet us in Salina," Paco said. "Know what day it is?"

"I figure we pretty much used up the month of May. Maybe less'n a week left of it."

"That would mean we will beat the deadline."

"Yup. A dollar more a head."

"Maybe two," Paco said.

"Did you figger how many head we lost back there?"

"No. Twenty or thirty, perhaps," Paco said.

"More than a dozen, I figger."

"The head count will be close."

The cattle moved at a good pace. The trail to Salina was well marked. Paco sent Curly Bob ahead to scout for Kiowa or more farmers with shotguns or pitchforks. They saw a few farms along the way and curious children walked out to stare at the cattle and throw rocks until they were chased off by the outriders.

They had lost two men in the fight at the

river. Joadie Lee and Bernie James. They could have lost more, Paco reasoned, but the decision to start crossing the river while it was still dark had probably saved a number of lives.

Mainly, he told Roy, they had lucked out because Jared had shot the leader, Pete Boggs, and killed him.

"He was the bastard," Paco said.

"Yeah, that man didn't have no quit in him, for sure."

They bedded the herd down late at night. The men gnawed on jerky and cold beans, apricots. There was no hot coffee, but nobody grumbled. They knew they were close to Salina and there would be payday and soft beds at the end of the trail.

Paco and Roy saw to it that the hands kept their optimism at a high level.

Two days later, on the third day after leaving the river crossing, the herd came in sight of Salina. The outriders whooped and hollered to see the buildings and townspeople riding out to see them.

They cheered even louder when Doc Blaine rode up to Paco, Roy, and Al with a wide grin on his face.

"Howdy, boys," he said. "You'll be happy to know that it's the twenty-eighth day of May and that means we're going to get fifteen dollars a head for these fine cattle you brung."

"Ain't that the goin' price in Abilene?" Roy said.

"Sometimes, sometimes," Doc said.

"How is Jared?" Paco asked.

Doc's chest swelled with a deep breath. "I don't know yet. I got him a sawbones and he was awake when I left him. Miles is stickin' to him like seed ticks on a bull's balls."

"But you think he is going to be all right," Paco said.

"That boy has more gumption than a Tennessee snake oil drummer," Doc said. "I'm countin' on him to pull through."

None of the men mentioned Caroline's name, but she was on their minds. They knew from Norm Collins what Earl Rawson had done to her.

"Just follow me to the stockyards, boys," Doc said, and turned Sandy toward town. He couldn't wait to see the look on Mr. Albert Fenster's face when he saw over three thousand head of Texas cattle fill up the corrals at the railhead.

He had heard about the fight at the river crossing from Miles and Will.

But it was Jared he was worried about and he would not linger long at the yards. Just long enough to get a final tally and present his bill of lading to Fenster.

He rode to the stock pens like a conquering general, his head held high, Sandy prancing like a parade horse in a single-footed gait. If Jared pulled through and his sons shook hands in a show of filial friendship, his triumph would be complete.

And this night, he knew, Salina, Kansas, would know that good men from Texas were in town with their pockets full of money and the widest grins in Kansas on their faces.

CHAPTER 33

Dr. William Aiken, a surgeon in his late forties with graying muttonchop sideburns, close-set pale blue eyes, a prosperous paunch, and small delicate hands, listened intently to Jared's heartbeat. He moved the stethoscope over the heart on either side, then to Jared's back. He finished his examination and let the instrument dangle against his white coat.

"Far as I can tell, Mr. Blaine," he said, "your heart is sound."

Aiken ran a finger over the healing wound on Jared's chest. He had removed the few stitches around one section of the wound a few moments before.

"I feel fine, Doctor," Jared said. "No pain."

"You were lucky," Aiken said. "A small fragment of the soft lead bullet lodged in your top rib. It appears that the bullet itself was deflected, or it might have torn out your lung."

"I can go home now?" Jared asked.

Aiken smiled. "Put on your shirt. Your father and brother are in the waiting room."

"Thanks, Doctor," Jared said. He put on his shirt and stepped down off the examination table, followed Aiken out of his office and into the waiting room of the St. John's Infirmary in Salina, Kansas.

Doc and Miles saw him and got up off the bench. Norm Collins rose from his chair, his mouth spread in a wide grin that showed his tobacco-stained teeth.

Doc embraced Jared as Miles looked on. Jared squeezed his father.

He looked past him at Miles, a warm twinkle in his eyes. Miles was not smiling, but was wan and pale, with a worried look on his face.

"Pa," Jared said. "Thanks." He broke his embrace and stepped over to Miles.

"I owe you my life, brother," he said.

Miles was speechless.

"I mean it," Jared said. "Will told me what you did. I'm mighty obliged."

"Let's get out of here," Doc said. "A bunch of the boys are waiting to see you, Jared. They're all over at the Red Dog Saloon."

Jared looked over at Norm, who stood, hat in hand, a foot away, his eyebrows arched as if he were waiting to ask a question.

Jared recognized him and walked over.

"Norm, how come you're here?" he asked.

"Well, your pa and Miles, they asked me to come. I guess I got something to tell you."

"Can it wait? I'm plumb parched and the boys are waiting for me."

Miles stepped up to the two men.

"It can't wait, Jared," he said. "It's about Caroline. Tell him, Norm. Tell him all of it."

"Let's get out of here," Doc said. He pointed to the door and the others followed him past the reception desk and out onto the street.

As they walked along, Norm told Jared about Earl Rawson and what he had done to Caroline, how he and Skeeter had taken her by wagon to the Slash B, where his mother and father had taken care of her.

"She's in a nursing home, Jared, where you can see her when we get back to Amarillo."

Jared was stunned to a dumbstruck silence. They walked slowly down the street with its small shops and drab storefronts proclaiming a section of town that was older than the rest.

"Caroline is mad?" he said, a layer of bewilderment in his tone.

"No, Jared. They say that boy, when he beat her, did something to her brain."

"I can't believe it," Jared said. "My beautiful Caroline."

Miles cleared his throat, hawked up a gob of phlegm, and spat off the boardwalk.

Jared glanced at Miles. "Sorry," he said. "I forgot she was your wife, Miles."

"That's all right, Jared. She belongs to all of us now. All we can do is see that she gets good care and lives a good long life."

"I'd like to get my hands on that kid, Rawson," Jared said. "When I let you hire him off me, Miles, I thought it was good riddance. But I never thought he'd beat up on Caroline."

"None of us did, Jared," Miles said.

"You don't have to worry none about Rawson no more," Norm said. He was a step behind the Blaines.

"How come?" Jared asked. He stopped and turned to face Collins. Miles and Doc stopped too.

"Skeeter rode up from Amarillo," Norm said. "Got here last night. Seems he had some news about Rawson."

"Go ahead, Norm," Miles said. "Tell him."

"Skeeter said Rawson wore his horse out lighting a shuck for Fort Worth. He got roaring drunk there and stole a horse from a rancher named Bert Finwoodie."

"Didn't we buy some whitefaces from Finwoodie a long while back?" Jared said.

"Yep, we did," Doc said. "But let Norm tell you the rest of it, Jared."

"Bert got some hands together and they tracked Rawson to Dallas, where the boy took up with a woman of ill repute. They grabbed him and took him back to Fort Worth, where a judge heard the case and ordered Rawson to be hanged. They hanged him right off. Bert heard about what Rawson did to Caroline and rode over to Amarillo and told your ma, who told Skeeter to hightail it for Salina and tell Doc. I seen Skeeter first and got the story first and I told Doc. Now I'm tellin' you, Jared. Rawson is dead and you don't have to worry about him no more."

Jared's eyes filled with tears. His father put a hand on Jared's shoulder. Miles put an arm around his brother's waist and squeezed. He started to weep as well, and then Doc's eyes leaked tears. Norm stood there, his head bowed out of respect.

"I guess," Jared said, "that's some justice for your Caroline, Miles."

"For *our* Caroline, Jared," Miles said.

Jared looked at his brother. He smiled through his tears and then he put his arms around his father and brother and they walked toward the Red Dog Saloon, Norm following a few steps behind.

To his surprise, tears came to Norm's eyes as well.

Later, he would tell Skeeter and the others about this, saying, "I never thought I'd see the day."

"Tragedy has a way of bringin' folks together," Skeeter would say, and all the men would nod knowingly at such a profound statement.

At the saloon, Doc bought a round of drinks for all hands.

Then Miles and Jared chipped in together and bought more rounds.

The men from the Rocking M, the Slash B, and the Lazy J bought the next round and toasted the Blaines. The Kansas onlookers in the saloon joined in, with their free drinks in hand, without knowing what the Texans were celebrating.

One of them said, however, "Boy, them Texans sure know how to have a hell of a time."

And they all had a hell of a time at the Red Dog that afternoon, even after Albert Fenster and Alvin Mortenson joined them to offer Doc a new contract for the following spring.

A while later, Miles walked to the bar and spoke to the barkeep. The bartender reached down and brought up a large round box.

Miles carried the box to his table and set it in front of Jared.

"What's this?" Jared asked.

"It's a hatbox," Curly Bob said in a loud voice.

"Open it, Jared," Miles said.

Jared opened the box and pulled out a brand-new Stetson.

"You can thank the boys for that," Doc said.

Jared put on the hat, squared it, and tamped on the crown.

"What do you know?" he said. "It fits."

Everyone laughed and cheered as the drinks kept coming.

"How did you get the right size?" Jared asked his father.

"Miles put on a bunch of hats. That was the one that fit him."

Jared looked at Miles and smiled, his eyes filling with a soft mist. He doffed his hat and bowed to Miles.

"I guess this proves it," Jared said. "You and me are true brothers."

And all the hands raised a mighty cheer.

ABOUT THE AUTHOR

Ralph Compton stood six foot eight without his boots. He worked as a musician, a radio announcer, a songwriter, and a newspaper columnist. His first novel, *The Goodnight Trail,* was a finalist for the Western Writers of America Medicine Pipe Bearer Award for Best Debut Novel. He was also the author of the *Sundown Riders* series and the *Border Empire* series.

The employees of Thorndike Press hope you have enjoyed this Large Print book. All our Thorndike, Wheeler, and Kennebec Large Print titles are designed for easy reading, and all our books are made to last. Other Thorndike Press Large Print books are available at your library, through selected bookstores, or directly from us.

For information about titles, please call:
  (800) 223-1244

or visit our Web site at:
  http://gale.cengage.com/thorndike

To share your comments, please write:
Publisher
Thorndike Press
10 Water St., Suite 310
Waterville, ME 04901